MW01483247

The Mormon Mountain Meadows Massacre

From the Diary of Captain John I. Ginn

By

Steven E. Farley

ISBN: 1-4107-4365-9 (e-book)
ISBN: 1-4107-4364-0 (Paperback)
ISBN: 1-4107-4363-2 (Dust Jacket)

Library of Congress Control Number: 2003092377

This book is printed on acid free paper.

Printed in the United States of America
Bloomington, IN

1stBooks - rev. 04/22/03

SPECIAL THANKS

To: Yale University Collection of Western Americana, Beinecke Rare Book and Manuscript Library. For their help on publication rights.

To: Utah State Historical Society, Utah History Information Center. For their help and research for publication rights.

To: Rev. Larry Preston from Butte, Montana, for the information on his Great-great Grandfather Mr. James Gemmell, and what his Grandfather over heard in Brigham Young's office, about three weeks before the Massacre. (Chapter X.)

MORMON AND INDIAN WARS;

THE MOUNTAIN MEADOWS MASSACRE,

AND OTHER TRAGEDIES AND TRANSACTIONS

INCIDENT TO THE MORMON REBELLION OF 1857.

TOGETHER WITH THE PERSONAL RECOLLECTIONS OF A

CIVILIAN WHO WITNESSED MANY OF THE HORRIFYING SCENES

DESCRIBED.

BY

CAPTAIN JOHN I. GINN

The months and weeks roll on,
you wonder-did I make the right decision,
you're fine in the morning,
by evening you are no more.

ABOUT THE DIARY OF CAPTAIN JOHN I. GINN.

Captain John I. Ginn in 1857 at the age of 21 came west from Missouri, in Route to California. On his way west he kept a diary of his travels and even used various pieces of scraps of paper to write on. In the diary he tells everything that he witnessed in Utah and of the Mountain Meadows Massacre with great reference to details (Ginn served as an apprentice printer in Montgomery, Alabama for a local newspaper).

The original papers, on which Ginn had written out these various details of his experiences and knowledge of what had transpired during the period of the Mormon and Indian Wars, the Mountain Meadows Massacre and the Mormon Rebellion against the authority of the United States Government, were given by him to his family.

In about 1920 the Ginn Diary and papers were given to a book publisher in Salt Lake City, Utah. The publisher was afraid to publish this diary, because of the repercussions that might have occurred after its publication in the State of Utah (We believe it was the Shepard Book Publishing Co.) The diary was put into manuscript form and was given to J. Cecil Alter about 1924-1925. (It is unknown how the publisher came by the diary.)

This manuscript was owned by J. Cecil Alter, author of *Jim Bridger* and celebrated Utah historian. Alter, in an original signed letter dated April 26th, 1950, (this letter is in the "authors" personal collection along with the only carbon copy of the only book that Alter had bound up in red buckram, leather label, gilt for the sum of $125.00 by Wm. F. Kelleher of New Jersey.) In the letter Alter says: "About twenty-five years ago Captain Ginn's manuscript and papers were submitted to a book publisher, acquaintance of mine, (The one Above) who had the material edited and retyped for possible publication in book form. But, for business reasons, it was not published and the principal typed copy, along with the original papers, were returned to the family.

This complete copy, herewith is the carbon copy, preserved for reference, and possible future use; but it has never been published. The Ginn family and relatives have disappeared in the intervening years, and their address is unknown". Signed J. C. Alter.

Alter, also an official historian for the State of Utah and with the Utah Historical Society did not want to publish this manuscript because of his social standing within the state.

Alter goes on to say in another document, that he thinks the Ginn family probably destroyed the original manuscripts, for they were of no interest, to them.

GINN-GENEALOGY

John I. Ginn: Born 1837	Married: 16 Nov 1871
Wife: Katie Musser: Born: 1854	Married: 16 Nov 1871 Birth Place: CA
Daughter: Dawn: Born 10 July 1872	Died 20 May 1873 Birth Place: Virginia City, Storey-County, NV
Son: Hay Ginn: Born 8 Sept. 1873	Birth Place: Virginia City, Storey-County, NV
Son: George Ginn: Born: 1876	Birth Place: Virginia City, Storey-County, NV

John I. Ginn: Worked for the following.

1866-1867 Territorial Enterprise-Virginia City, NV.

1868-1869 Reno Evening Gazette-as a printer.

EDITOR-OWNER

1870-1900 Nevada State Journal-------------- Humbolot Co. NV

1871 Carson Daily Register-------------------- Humbolot Co. NV

1872 Chronicle---------------------------------- Humbolot Co. NV

1872 Gold Hill News--------------------------- Humbolot Co. NV

1874 Virginia Indepent------------------------- Humbolot Co. NV

1874 Daily Independent------------------------ Humbolot Co. NV

1879 Peoples Advocate------------------------ Humbolot Co. NV

1880 Daily and Weekly Bodie Standard------Mono. Co. CA

On Nov 1871-John Inherited $1,000,000.00 in silver Stocks.

PREFACE

Nearly everyone who has read western history knows something about the Mountain Meadows massacre, which took place in southern Utah in September 7th-11th, 1857. Most of the facts connected with that episode have long since been made public. However, a diary with some papers, were discovered in 1920 which may shed some new light on the affair, and is particularly interesting to readers of this novel. It shows that except for the treachery of a Mormon guide, a company of Texans would have rescued an unfortunate party of emigrants. To those who are not familiar with the details, the story will be briefly renewed for you.

The emigrants who comprised the Mountain Meadows party were chiefly from Arkansas, with a few from Missouri, Illinois and Ohio. The Captain of their train was Alexander Fancher, from Ohio. An old mountaineer named Perkins, probably George Perkins who had trapped with Bill Williams, was guiding them. They started from the Missouri River in the spring of 1857, bound for California. Most of them were moderately well-to-do, and their equipment was of the best. There were 136 persons in the company, including men, women and children.

Due to the atrocities committed by the Mormons on emigrants passing through Utah, the government had started an army westward to protect overland travel. Brigham Young, a Mormon prophet, defied the government, declared a state of war, organized his private army, and prepared to give battle to the United States troops. As part of his plan, he issued an order that no emigrants might pass through Utah without his written permission.

At the time that order was issued, the Arkansas emigrants were already on their way south from (Zion) Salt Lake City on the Southern Route to California, which passed through the Mountain Meadows, about 50 miles west of Cedar City, Utah. They had no knowledge of the order, and knew of no reason why they should ask Brigham's permission to cross the desert. But their fine wagons and good cattle and horses excited the cupidity of the Mormons, who determined to destroy them and seize their goods, using the impending state of war as a pretext.

There was at that time good pasture at the Mountain Meadows, so the party decided to rest their oxen for a few days before passing over the barren deserts to the south. While camped there, the Mormons planned their execution. The original plan was to get the Indians to do the dirty work; but after a few volleys from the sharp-shooting emigrants the Indians retired and refused to go through with it. Then the Mormon militia took up the bloody business where the Indians had left off. Through the foulest treachery they persuaded the emigrants to give up their arms. When that had been done, they were marched single file away from their camp, the men in one group, the women and children in another. At the command of a Mormon bishop, the militia began firing and did not cease until every person in the entire company was dead, with the exception of sixteen small children. This massacre, performed by religious fanatics, was without question the bloodiest, blackest, foulest deed ever committed on American soil.

On the trail to California, and only a short distance behind the Arkansas party, was a company of Texans. Unfortunately we know very little about them. The only record available is the diary of Captain John I. Ginn. Captain Ginn, then a young man, was on his way to California, and bought passage with a company of refugees from Utah, passing through the Mountain Meadows three weeks after the massacre, before any of the bodies had been buried. In his diary he says that this company of Texans, who were mostly frontiersmen, passed through Salt Lake City only a few days after the Mountain Meadows company, and were hurrying to join them before they left the settlements of Utah and entered the Nevada desert. It may be that they suspected treachery, and hoped to strengthen the other party, which contained many women and children.

At any rate, the Texans started south, traveling rapidly. At Fillmore, they were induced to hire a Mormon guide, Jacob Hamblin, who knew all the trails, and who also knew what was to take place at the Mountain Meadows. It was a mistake, a fatal mistake, for the Arkansas emigrants. Instead of following the well-known trail, Hamblin guided these Texans around the scene of the massacre, down

Black Canyon, a very difficult trail over which no wagons had previously passed. As near as can be determined the Texans passed south of Cedar City on the very day the massacre took place at the Mountain Meadows.

After getting out of Black Canyon, the Texans hurried on, hoping each day to meet with the Arkansas company. Hamblin left them after his mission had been performed. When they again struck the main trail south of the Meadows they found that no wagons had passed recently. They presumed that the Arkansas Company had stopped to rest their oxen somewhere along the road and would overtake them in a few days. They continued on until they reached San Bernardino, California, the end of the emigrant trail, where they waited two weeks for the Arkansas Company to arrive. When nothing was heard of them, the Texans organized a scouting party of eleven men to return over the trail and find out what had become of their friends.

This party of eleven Texans rode east into Nevada, until they met the little company with which Captain Ginn was traveling. Ginn told them of the horrible sights he had seen at Mountain Meadows, and that the entire company had been wiped out. With such small numbers there was nothing the Texans could do but turn back with the sad news.

Most of the Texas emigrants had gone on to Los Angeles by that time. Captain Ginn wrote a description of what he had seen for a Los Angeles newspaper. When they learned all the facts, the Texans were so incensed at the bloody deed that they organized a small army of twenty-five men and started for San Bernardino, with the intention of wiping out the Mormon colony which had been planted there several years before.

When Brigham Young found himself face to face with the United States army, he sent out an urgent call for every Mormon outside Utah to return and help fight the government. San Bernardino was the largest Mormon outpost at the time, and a large number of men prepared to return to Utah. Their departure was greatly hastened when they heard that the Texans were coming to take revenge for the Mountain Meadows massacre.

That bloody deed has passed into history, where it will forever be a stain on the history of Utah and the records of the Mormon Church.

But it is interesting to speculate on what might have happened, had those Texans arrived at the Mountain Meadows at the time of the massacre. It is extremely doubtful if any of those brave Mormons, who shot down unarmed men and defenseless women and children, would have survived that day.

Retribution would have been visited on them before their bloody hands were dry. The sly Mormon guide knew what might happen, and so guided them away from the bloody ground. If they had disregarded his advice and used their own judgment, the blackest deed in American history might have been avoided.

Mormon records are absolutely silent on this Texas Party. The Texans passed through Salt Lake City after the Arkansans, when Mormon feeling against outsiders was at high pitch, yet they were not molested in any way. They spurned the idea of obtaining Brigham Young's permission to pass through the territory, and the Mormon cowards, who did not dare face armed men, let them pass without molestation. With all odds in their favor, the Mormons were afraid of the handful of Texans.

The great pity is that these, fighting Texans did not reach Mountain Meadows in time. If they had, they would have changed the history of Utah, and the Mormon Church would not now be trying to live down and forget the bloodiest episode in western history.

A DESTROYING ANGEL

Authors Collection

Photo about 1885

Pinkley Weaver (about age 64) with Indian wife from the (Hupa tribe) in Lewiston, California.

Weaver was one of the Destroying Angels at the Mountain Meadows Massacre. His brother Dallas Weaver was killed in this Massacre on Sept. 10th, 1857.

To Whom It May Concern:

What I have written on this and other matters that came under my observation during the tragic year of 1857 has not been shaded by any prejudice I have against the Mormon religion, nor by any bias I might feel in favor of any other form of irrational superstition.

Captain John I. Ginn

CHAPTER I

Personal Recollection of Captain John I. Ginn.

I left Independence, Mo. in June 1857, as a member of William Magraw's Pacific Wagon Road Expedition, which moved up by Leavenworth and thence west along the California emigrant road through Kansas, Nebraska and Wyoming to Utah. Captain Ana of the regular army was our paymaster, Dr. Cooper of the army, our surgeon, and Colonel (afterward General) Fred W. Lander was our Chief Engineer. Several young graduates from West Point accompanied Colonel Lander as assistant engineers, and the Smithsonian Institution sent with us a German naturalist whom the boys designated the "Bug Catcher."

Passing over many little serio-comic incidents of camp life and the fitting out of a large wagon train for the plains, I start in at old Fort Kearney, Nebraska, near which the first tragedy occurred, and where a party were burying a Boston man named Sanburn, who had been shot dead by hostile Cheyenne Indians during a raid upon one of the beef cattle droves near Plum Creek.

Just across the road from the little military post-called Fort Kearney, 400 Pawnee Indians from Kansas were encamped. This was then on the margin of the buffalo range and in those days buffalo by the millions overran those western plains. These Pawnees had come out to lay in a winter supply of jerked buffalo meat, and had camped near the military post for protection to their families from the Cheyennes, then a very numerous and hostile tribe, and they were just as murderous toward the civilized tribes of their own race as they were toward the whites.

Our party passed by the post about one mile and then turned off to the right and went into camp down on the Platte River bottom, where we remained two nights. Late into the afternoon of the day we were in this camp a party of fourteen men in the employ of the great freighting firm of Russell, Majors & Waddell went into camp near the right bank of the Platte river, near Plum Creek, some twenty odd miles further west. They had several wagons loaded with supplies, and had in charge about 800 head of fat beef cattle they were driving out to deliver to the army then en route to Utah to put down the rebellious and hostile Mormons. While their conduct proved these men to be the bravest of the brave, most of them were unused to the wiles of hostile Indians.

While they were attending to camp affairs, cooking, eating, etc, hundreds of armed Cheyennes walked into their camp, while other hundreds on horseback quietly surrounded the grazing and equally unsuspecting cattle, preparatory to stampeding and running them off. These men, not being plainsmen and having just passed through hundreds of friendly Indians at Fort Kearney, never dreamed that the red devils mingling with them had any designs upon them until one young buck climbed upon the tongue of a wagon to investigate and helped himself to the contents of the vehicle.

The unfortunate Sanburn took hold of the Indian and promptly pulled him down from the wagon tongue, when the red devil promptly pulled a pistol and shot Sanburn dead. In an instant the firing became general. The men quickly gathered behind the wagons for protection, while the Indians fell behind a low embankment into the dry bed of an old slough. The men, and especially two McCarty brothers who were dead shots and destitute of fear, poured a galling fire into the red skins-so much so that on the following day many pools of blood were found in the slough. Finally a large, manly looking Kentuckian named Robb, of the party, fell helpless with his right thigh bone shattered by a rifle ball. His companion picked him up and retreated to the breast-high bank of the river, and under this protection they started to make their way back to Fort Kearney, sometimes on the wet sand under the bank and sometimes in the shallow marginal water of the river.

The Indians then rifled the wagons of their contents, and drove the 800 head of beef cattle off south and over the hills toward Walnut Creek. A considerable number of the Indians followed, as near as they dared to, the white men down near the river until after dark and then a portion of them (they were all mounted) crossed to the north bank of the river and the men could hear them running their horses down the stream, evidently to re-cross and ambuscade them.

Then the whites left the river-bank and struck out across the grassy plain to strike the wagon road to the fort. Meantime one of their own mules, a gentle and faithful animal, that had stampeded when the firing began in camp, came to them on the bank of the river. On this providential visitor, without bridle or saddle, they placed Robb of the shattered thigh, and told him to ride to Fort Kearney, where he was placed under treatment of the post surgeon, and I afterward learned that he recovered and returned home.

Another thing that brings back the horrors of that night with great vividness was one of those worse than tropic rainfalls, accompanied by deafening thunder and frequent and vivid flashes of lightning that lighted up the whole horizon as bright as sunlight. Our wagons were all closed with covers and we were sleeping on the ground under them, but our whole camp was flooded to a depth of four inches, and we had to gather up our bedding and climb up on the wagon tongues, where we sat until daylight.

The next morning, accompanied by 10 soldiers of the fifty stationed at Kearney, and with the remaining twelve men fully armed (for some of them had failed to get hold of their arms in the sudden and unexpected attack), all under the command of Jim Rupe, a brave and resourceful plainsman, the party started for the Plum Creek camp to bury Sanburn and try to recover the cattle. We also broke camp that morning and started west.

We had eighty-three well-armed men and were not afraid of an attack from the hostiles, and never were attacked, although we traveled through 400 miles of country over which the hostile Cheyennes roamed. As we passed the Plum Creek camp late in the afternoon, this party was engaged in burying Sunburn and, seeing no Indians in the vicinity, we drove on up the Platte about four miles and went into camp, subsequently we learned that the little party had followed the trail of the cattle and Indians into the Walnut Creek hills and there surprised and fired upon a large band of the hostiles, killing a number of them and recovering about sixty head of the stolen cattle.

In the same summer of 1857, Col. Edwin V. Summer (afterward General Summer, killed in the battle of South Mountain, MD.) was out after the Cheyennes with a large force of cavalry, infantry and artillery. At the crossing of the South Platte (where the town of Julesberg now stands) we came upon the wagon train of Colonel

Summer, under guard of about 100 soldiers and about 400 friendly Sioux Indians, who were encamped on the same grounds. Colonel Summer had started out with a light pack train carrying eight days' rations for his men, and had then been gone thirty-two days, without a word of his movements or whereabouts having reached the officer of the wagon train guard.

Shortly after our arrival at Fort Laramie, situated on the river of the same name, near its confluence with the North Platte, a Cheyenne sub-chief spent a night in some Indian lodges just across the Laramie river from the post, and reported that Summer had overtaken a large force of the Cheyennes near where Cherry Creek empties into the South Platte (where the city of Denver, Colo. now stands), and after a hotly contested battle had stampeded the Indians, killing about 800 of them and capturing and destroying all their winter supplies. As many more of them starved to death during the following winter, this battle broke both the power and the spirit of the Cheyennes, and they sued for peace and got it, although a few years after some small bands of renegades of the tribe began raiding the border settlements and kept it up until the remnant of this once powerful and warlike tribe was rounded up and placed upon a reservation in the Indian Territory.

When we left the white settlements General Harney was under orders to take command of the army then being mobilized to put down the Mormon rebellion and, until after I was taken prisoner by the Mormon army late in the autumn of that year, no one connected with either the military or wagon road expeditions knew that, in consequence of the renewal of the sectional troubles in Kansas (in which I had participated in the summer of 1856) this order had been countermanded and that Col. Albert Sidney Johnston (afterward killed while in command of the Confederate Army in the Battle of Shiloh) had been ordered to the command of the army sent out to put down the Mormons.

Colonel Albert Johnston (killed at the battle of Shiloh 1862.) was then engaged in running the boundary line between Arkansas and Kansas and, in consequences of this change, the commander did not reach the army till well along in the winter. Meantime the 10th Infantry, under Colonel Alexander, and recruited up to 1,100 men, the

Fifth Infantry, 1,000 strong, under Lieutenant Colonel Carlos Waite, and one field and one siege battery of artillery under Captain Reno (afterward General Reno, killed at the battle of South Mountain, Md.) had been dispatched across the plains to await the arrival of the commander on the border of the enemy's country.

A regiment of dragoons had been detained at Fort Leavenworth to escort the commander to the front, and this left the advancing army without mounted men to protect its front, rear and flanks, and in consequence it met with many and serious losses in horses, cattle and other supplies captured or destroyed by the Mormon cavalry.

Foreseeing that the Magraw expedition was going into winter quarters in the wind River Valley, near the foot of Fremont's Peak in the heart of the Rocky Mountains, with barely sufficient provisions to last for two months, and knowing that no others supplies could reach us for six or eight months, I quit the expedition at Fort Laramie, obtained employment with Captain Clarke, Regimental commissary with the Tenth Infantry (the advance regiment), and remained with that regiment until it moved camp several times up the valley of Ham's Fork of Green River, north of the road. The first demonstration made against the army by the Mormons occurred at Pacific Springs, where we went into camp on the evening of the day we crossed the continental divide through the South Pass. Here the regimental camp and baggage wagons were grouped about the springs proper, while the commissary and forage trains were drawn up in a long line stretching away to the southwest between the little stream and the road, the wagons standing side by side, about twenty feet apart, with their tongues almost reaching the road. I was sleeping under one of the wagons of the corn train, and during the night the whole camp was awakened by a terrific yelling and firing by six mounted Mormons who dashed down the road, stampeding every horse and mule in the camp. Here was a plight for a whole regiment to be placed in, without a mule to move a wagon.

There was a camp of guards some 150 yards to the northwest of camp, on high ground, but as the intruders had slipped in quietly from the northeast the guards dare not fire on them when they opened the racket, as their shots would be directed toward the tents of their own comrades. The Mormons were firing in the air, their object being to frighten the mules, and not a shot was fired at them during their passing raid. The camp was greatly alarmed and the whole regiment was soon drawn up under arms. The mules ran about three miles when their feet ceased to clatter on the hard, smooth road, their Mormon leaders having slowed down and stopped them. Then Colonel Alexander ordered the buglers to sound the "stable call" as loud as they could.

The mules had come to know this call to eat, and the clear, ringing notes of the bugle had scarcely died away when the heels of the mules could be heard hitting the road again. Directly they came dashing into camp in a bunch, together with six additional animals wearing saddles and bridles-the whole Mormon mount.

Porter Rockwell, Chief of the Destroying Angels or Danites, with whom I afterward became quite intimate, told me that he was in (and he probably planned) the Pacific Springs raid; that four of his party dashed on ahead in order to slow down, round up and keep together the stampeded mules, while himself and one companion fell back to bring up the rear and urge on any laggard mules. He said that about one mile out from the army camp himself and his companion had occasion to ride out and dismount in the sagebrush a few steps from the road.

His comrades in the lead, after getting the mules quieted, had also dismounted to await the arrival of Rockwell and his companion, not knowing what might have happened to them. While thus standing idle in the road, the stable call rang out on the still night air when every mule of the 2,000 raised its head, listened a moment and then wheeled about and started back toward the camp as fast as his legs could carry him. The animals of the dismounted Mormons also jerked loose from their owner and joined the flying procession, and as they passed Rockwell and his companion their saddle animals also broke away and joined the returning column, It was now the Mormon raiders instead of the army who were in a sorry plight.

The next day the 10th Infantry made a long, hard march to the Little Sandy, where we went into camp at dark near the stream on a grassy flat overgrown with mesquite trees. Porter Rockwell afterward told me that himself and his dismounted companions rushed on foot the same night they lost their mules and took to the mesquite brush on the Little Sandy some three or four miles below the road, with the purpose of stealthily creeping up on the night the army should camp there and stealing a remount; that when they saw the army come down from the high plain to the stream the next night they got ready to execute their purpose. Waiting until well along in the night, they crept quietly up stream through the mesquite until suddenly they came upon a bunch of horses already saddled but picketed out and grazing.

Thinking these were the saddle horses of the army officers they hurriedly secured fifteen of them, mounted and pushed on that night to the Big Sandy, where they knew they would find a force of Mormon cavalry. Arriving at the Big Sandy camp just after daylight, the commander came out, took a look at the horses and their equipment and exclaimed; "How in the name of heaven did you come into possession of the horses of our comrades who went over to the Little Sandy day before yesterday to see what they could do toward crippling the army of invasion?"

Here was another "situation" the first raiders had stolen the horses of the second raiders and left them a-foot in a bleak region a long way from help or home. In consequence of this mistake neither our stock nor our camp were disturbed on the Little Sandy, and the next night we encamped on the Big Sandy, but of coarse the Mormon cavalry had moved on. The next day the 10th Infantry marched over to Green River, where we were to lay over one day-for the army rested every eighth day.

However, on the afternoon of our rest day at Green River a courier arrived with a note to Colonel Alexander urgently requesting him to push on that night to Ham's Fork, where seven of the heavy provision trains had been sent out, Russell, Majors & Waddell were massed and were being menaced by the Mormons. The threatened trains, which were under the protection only of the teamsters and a small squad of soldiers (under Lieutenant Deshler) who had been detached from the escort of Captain Van Vliet on the return of that officer from Salt Lake Valley, where he had been dispatched earlier in the season to prepare winter quarters for the army. Colonel Alexander at once gave orders to have everything ready to move promptly, rapidly and silently as possible at dark.

At that time, besides the numerous heavy supply trains assembled at Ham's Fork, each train consisting of twenty-six wagons, there was one train in camp at the Big Sandy, one at Green River and another on the high divide between Green River and Ham's Fork.

My mess, consisting of nine mounted men (besides a cook) was engaged in driving the beef cattle then with the army. Promptly at dark the 10th Regiment took the road, followed by the several wagon trains, and we rounded up the beef cattle and started them off. By this time the cattle had become so well trained and so accustomed to following the wagon trains that we had no trouble with them whatever. They would keep close up to the rear of the (corn) train though we might be three miles behind or off the road hunting. On this night we were riding along leisurely, not realizing how rapidly the army was moving on a forced march, so that when we passed through the train on the divide, about midnight, we were fully four miles behind the regiment. Soon after we passed through it a force of Mormon Cavalry under Bill Hickman descended upon it, set fire to the wagons, which consumed them and their contents. Hickman soon afterwards told me in Salt Lake city that his force stood in a cedar forest half a mile south of the road when the regiment and its wagon trains passed, and that he started to fire the train when he heard horses' hooves coming up from Green River, when he turned back under cover and waited until a small squad of mounted men (which was myself and my eight companions) passed. The same night or early next morning Hickman's and other Mormon cavalry burned up the two large supply trains at Green River and Big Sandy, thus depriving the army of about 500,000 pounds of provisions intended for its maintenance during the long and severe winter then setting in.

As the 10th Infantry marched down the slope into the beautiful valley of Ham's Fork, where the supply trains were huddled together and their position fortified as effectively as possible, we could see on the road from Fort Bridger beyond a cloud of dust kicked up by a column of 500 mounted Mormon coming to attack them. Seeing the army approaching, the Mormons turned off to the right, crossed Black's Fork and presumably returned to Fort Bridger.

A day or two afterward Reno's artillery and the 5th Infantry came up and the whole army continued in camp along Ham's Fort for some weeks; moving up the stream occasionally as the grass was eaten out. Winter was coming on, several snow squalls had occurred, but the grazing was still good, and no commander nor cavalry had yet come out, and the Mormon Cavalry continued to hover about and occasionally stampede the cattle or mules and to pick up and carry off a soldier or teamster who had strayed away in search of sage hens, or rabbits. The inertia of camp life, the knowledge that the whole command would soon have to go on greatly reduced rations, the danger to hunting parties and the rapid approach of cold weather, caused a good deal of unrest and uneasiness among both soldiers and citizens attached to the army. One day the chief officers of the several commands held a consultation and the report soon became current that they had decided that in case the commander did not arrive within a certain number of days they would attempt to make old Fort Hall (then in Oregon, but now in Idaho) and go into winter quarters. I had left the states with the intention of making my way to California, and I had no idea of going to Fort Hall, where I would have to spend the winter on quarter rations and still be further from California (in time) in the spring than I was when I left Independence Mo., the preceding spring.

So I decided to resign my position at once, draw what pay was due me, strike out on foot along the backbone of the range to old Fort Bridger and throw myself on the mercy of the Mormons. A young Kentucky boy named Joe Franks, about 19 years of age (I was then 21) determined to go with me. But he was enlisted as a teamster and would have to desert leaving his back pay. I could pass him out through the picket lines all right and did so, and for three days without food or water, we tramped through a snow-storm and over and through sagebrush, grass, greasewood, sand, rocks and roots. After dark on the evening of the third day, while trudging wearily along through light but drifting snow and scrubby greasewood scarcely five inches high, facing a bitter cold wind that was sweeping the high, bald divide north of Fort Bridger, we came in sight of the huge cottonwood fires of the Mormon troops in the valley of Black's Fork, near the Fort. Franks was almost exhausted, but I kept urging him on for nearly three hours more. And still the camp-fires appeared to be three or four miles off.

At last he wrapped his buffalo robe about him and fell upon the snow, remarking, “John, you go on; you have strength enough to save yourself, but I am gone anyhow, so leave me alone.” Almost instantly he fell asleep, which I knew would prove fatal within an hour unless I could get him warm. I wrapped my own bedding around him, brushed away a patch of snow and rolled him over on the dry ground. Then I put on a large pair of buffalo skin gauntlets and began pulling up little bunches of greasewood and putting it in piles along his back. These I set on fire and then kept pulling up more and making another line two feet off. As soon as one line would burn out (say, in six or eight minutes) I would roll him over upon the heated ground and set fire to another line. This I kept up until sunrise next morning, keeping myself fairly warm by exercise. At sunrise Joe Franks woke up greatly refreshed, while I was myself completely exhausted. Both of us were nearly famished, for water, and while we could see the Mormon camp was but two miles off, what pleased us more was a view of Black’s Fork, a clear, pure and beautiful mountain torrent splashing over the rocks within 300 feet of us. I have often thought since that, if I had known the evening before that beautiful stream was so near to me Joe Franks would have died on the mountain that night.

We both drunk as long as we could swallow, and then climbed to the top of the bluff and sat down on a ledge of rocks to rest ourselves in the warm morning sunshine. It was a perfect day, and the scene below and before us was one of picturesque beauty. Soon, however, we discovered there was tremendous commotion among the Mormon troops. They had been expecting an attack from the army, and mistook us for the advance scouts, supposing, as they afterward explained that the army had slipped by without being seen by their outriders. Directly 400 cavalry dashed across the river and down the valley far out at the eastward, so as to get a good view of the high plateau in the rear of our position, while 500 or 600 infantry with artillery ascended the mountain about one mile west of us, until they could view the high plateau and the Ham’s Fork road for some miles in our rear, and seeing no signs of an army back of us a Mormon

Captain and two other mounted men rode down to us and inquired who we were. I told him. He became very indignant that we had not proceeded directly to their headquarters and peremptorily ordered us to do so at once, which we did.

The Mormon commander at Fort Bridger was Colonel Thomas Collister, a Kentuckian, and an unusually kind and intelligent man for a religious fanatic. Upon our arrival at the post we reported to him. He took our firearms, under promise that they would be restored to us in Salt Lake City, which they never were, even a little pocket derringer belonging to Joe Franks, and with which he was a dead shot. Colonel Collister told us that, as he was expecting an attack from the army on Fort Bridger almost any day and did not want us in the way, he would send us over to Fort Supply, twelve miles south, where there had been a Mormon settlement, a saw-mill and a farm, cabbage, onions, potatoes and turnips being still in the ground, though the settlement had been abandoned, the mill dismantled and all the buildings and big log wagons or carts burned. Here, he assured us, we would be kindly treated as citizens, provided we did not prove to be spies by trying to escape to the army to give information of their situation and strength.

He then conducted us to the rear wall of the Bridger building (for every thing inflammable had been burned here on Oct. 3rd, 1857) pointed out plenty of beef and potatoes and told us to help ourselves. About noon an empty hay wagon returning to Fort Supply, accompanied by eight or ten armed and mounted Mormons, drew up at head-quarters, when Colonel Collister told us to get on the wagon, and that the first company relieved in the field to return to Salt Lake valley to rest he would send by and have us taken into the city. To the teamsters he simply said; "Tell Captain Bullock here are a couple of men, I have sent him." Upon our arrival at Fort Supply the teamster delivered this message literally.

Next morning after breakfast, however, Captain Bullock ordered some of his men to heat up one of those huge log-cart tires, cut it into sections about eight feet long, straighten out two sections and then bend one end of each in the form of a hook. Then he called up two burley-looking young Mormons, each armed with a shot gun, and ordered one of them to take Joe Franks out into the field and put him to digging potatoes and onions with "one of those hoes. "And the other to put me to digging turnips with the other "hoe" in another part of the field. My guard was an ignorant and very garrulous young Englishman of the lower class, wholly wrapped up in and saturated with Mormonism and the marvelous redemption of the world they were going to bring about. I agreed with him on every point, to all appearances. Arriving in the field where the succulent tubers were almost bursting from the ground, with my little 30-pound hoe I dug up about half a dozen, drew my pocket knife, sat down, peeled and ate them, for I always was fond of raw turnips, and I had not seen one before for a year, all the while keeping up a lively conversation with my guard, which seemed to please him greatly, as he seemed to think he was about adding to the glory of the "Kingdom" by adding a convert. I carried out this program until noon, and when we went to dinner I did not leave a single turnip exposed in the field. Arriving in camp for dinner I found Joe Franks' hands torn and bleeding from his too free use of the heavy wagon tire. I took him to one side and told him how smoothly I had been getting along and advised him to do likewise. He replied very sullenly; "Oh, the ignorant brute who is guarding me cannot talk anything but nonsense, and I would rather dig potatoes than listen to it"

After dinner I returned to my turnip eating. Late in the afternoon I saw a Mormon trooper riding around the field toward Fort Bridger, and asked my guard if that was the trooper's destination. He thought it was. I then asked him if he had any objection to me sending a written note to Colonel Collister. He said not, and hailed the trooper, while I tore a blank leaf from my diary and wrote Colonel Collister how we were being treated, suggesting that it did not comport with his promise to us. That night he dispatched a courier with an order to Captain Bullock to give us the freedom of the camp, exempt us from all camp duty and to treat us like gentleman. From that hour on we had a pleasant time, though I continued to visit the turnip patch two or three times a day to eat raw turnips, for I was vegetable hungry after nearly five months on the plains.

After the Mormons burned the three large supply trains on the road in the rear of the army, the work steers from those trains, aggregating nearly 1000 head, were driven on to the army camp on Ham's Fork to splice out the beef supply. As Colonel Johnston had not yet arrived with the Dragoons, the mounted Mormons continued to hover about and menace the army camps and their beef cattle. One windy day, while the army was encamped on the vast and dry grass plain on upper Ham's Fork with the cattle feeding below, one band of Mormons set a long line of fire across the plain above and to the windward of the camp, and while every available man and blanket was dispatched in that direction to fight the fire, another large band of mounted Mormons dashed in among the cattle below and drove them away in a hurry.

Joe Franks and myself had been prisoners at Fort Supply ten or twelve days when the Mormons arrived at Fort Bridger with the band of cattle, 1,000 or 1,200 head. True to his promise, Colonel Collister sent two mounted men to Fort Supply to escort Joe Franks and myself by a swampy, country road cut-off to join the cattle guards on the main road near the crossing of Bear River, some miles west of Bridger. As we had to go on foot, I, being a good walker, went on ahead leaving the two mounted guards with Joe Franks. Just as I reached the main road, at the top of the slope leading down to Bear River, and could hear the drivers yelling at the cattle in the distance, I came upon Porter Rockwell, Chief of the Destroying Angels, standing in the road with his arms and chin resting on the saddle of his favorite little mule. The recognition was mutual and instantaneous, for I had seen Rockwell early in the spring of that year (1857) when he came into Magraw's camp near Independence to enquire about some missing mules belonging to the Salt Lake mail line in which he was interested prior to its withdrawal, and he recognized me as "the boy had promptly protested against it," when Magraw ordered the men to hang him.

After a few inquiries and answers, Rockwell remarked that the ford at Bear River was rough, the current strong and the water cold, and then asked me to mount his mule and ride across to his camp on the opposite bank, remarking that he could jump on behind one of the boys driving the cattle and ride across himself. I rode across the river and up to the camp fire where four Mormons were cooking supper for the whole command.

Recognizing the mule and seeing it in possession of a stranger and a hated Gentile at that, they did not know what to make of it.

They were dumfounded, but looked daggers at me and, while I was hitching the mule, one of them picked up his gun, brought it to a ready and demanded sharply; "Where did you get that mule?" I told him, when he put down his gun and went on cooking. When Porter Rockwell arrived in camp he introduced me to the principal men of his command and after that I was treated with the greatest respect. After supper Rockwell took myself and Franks to one side and told us they desired to push the cattle a few miles further over that night to Yellow Creek to the camp of General Wells, the commander in chief of the Mormon army, and promised us a good supper there if we would assist by following behind in the road and pushing up the laggards while the mounted men would do the flanking and keep the cattle in the road. We did so and got the supper.

We reached the camp of General Wells about midnight and while Rockwell entered the General's tent Joe Franks and myself walked up to a large camp-fire to warm ourselves. While standing there one surly Mormon began abusing Gentiles in general and us in particular, when a South Carolina Mormon (a rare breed) struck the fellow across the head with a rifle, knocking him into the fire and across a large bed of live coals. Others sprang to the rescue and jerked the man from the fire, and just then Porter Rockwell ran out to see what the commotion was about and was closely followed by General Wells. The man with the gun explained that his comrade had insulted and started in to abuse the prisoners when he knocked him down, whereupon General Wells ordered the wounded man to the guard house and invited Joe Franks and myself to his own tent to spend the night.

The next day we moved on with the cattle, Rockwell proffering Franks and myself the finest dinner that could be gotten up in the city if we would help drive the cattle in. We gladly accepted the offer, as we had to follow Uncle Sam's cattle in anyway. At Cache Cave, at the head of Echo Canyon, we met a Mormon train going out with supplies for the army. Porter Rockwell overhauled it and distributed necessities and luxuries to his own command, giving Franks and myself an equal share with his own men. Passing down Echo Canyon, with its bristling fortification and great excavations made to flood the road and render it impassable, we reached its mouth at the Weber River, where Echo City on the Union Pacific Railroad now stands, where we found 1,600 Mormon troops encamped. Here we rested one day and then proceeded over the Big and Little Mountains, reaching Great Salt Lake City about noon. Rockwell gave us the promised dinner, and then we were released or allowed the freedom of the city so as to throw us upon our own expense.

Russell, Majors & Waddell

[In 1855, the Army awarded a two-year contract to William Russell, Alexander Majors, and William Waddell; the most experienced freighters of the time. The partnership hired 1,700 men as teamsters, purchased 7,500 head of oxen and 500 wagons. They established a field headquarters in the infant town of Leavenworth along with a blacksmith shop, wagon repair shop, lumberyard, meat processing plant and dry goods, outfitting, and grocery stores; helping the town to become firmly established in the Kansas Territory. In the summer of 1857, 48 wagon trains carrying almost four million pounds of goods were dispatched from Fort Leavenworth. An average wagon train consisted of 25 wagons each pulled by twelve oxen. The wagon master, whose word was law, commanded the train and about 30 teamsters. The teamsters never rode but actually walked along side the wagons, cracking their bullwhips to encourage the oxen and to snap off the heads of rattlesnakes along the trail. The loaded wagons moved at a rate of 10 to 15 miles per-day. Unloaded, they traveled about 20 miles per-day.]

CHAPTER II

The Mormon Reign of Terror.

Porter Rockwell, who conceived a genuine friendship for me, advised me not to put up at the Town House (the only hotel then in the city), as there were several Gentiles stopping there, and that they were all under more or less suspicion. I told him I was an utter stranger and could not know where to turn to find accommodation in a private house, whereupon he directed me to the home of "Mother Taylor", the mother of John Taylor of the Twelve Apostles, and afterward Brigham Young's successor as President of the Church. There I procured a comfortable room and good board at the family table, and there I remained until I left for California.

Old Mother Taylor was a kindly and rather intelligent old lady for a woman steeped to the eyes in Mormonism and believing with unquestioning credulity in every dogma, prophecy, and revelation put forth by the interested priesthood. She plied me with the literature of the church, the Book of Mormon, the Revelations of Joseph Smith, the Persecution of the Saints, etc., all of which were new and interesting to me but none of which had any more effect upon my analytical mind than water would have upon a duck's back for I had read equally absurd stories in equally sacred books gotten up by equally interested priesthood before. Old Father Taylor, then about 84, appeared to be a mere cipher about the house, though in accordance with the polygamous revelation he had taken unto himself two other wives- two old, shriveled up English maidens, apparently as old as himself, and who doubtless remained maidens till death.

Situated as I was in one of the oldest and most respected orthodox families of the church, and enjoying the conspicuous confidence and friendship of Porter Rockwell, Chief of the Destroying Angels and Brigham Young's confidential and most trusted Lieutenant, I was in a position to get a better insight into the workings of the Mormon mind and into the terrible and bloody methods then in vogue than was usually vouchsafed to a Gentile. Thus I was enabled to hear the inner and private opinion of many Mormon women on polygamy, and with what startling unanimity all classes endorsed the horrid and barbarous doctrine of "blood atonement" then being so vehemently preached and so cruelly and mercilessly practiced. But, while most of their barbarisms were copied from the Old Testament or history of the Jews in the days of the barbarism of the tribe, they found ample authority for the worse than savage doctrine of blood atonement in the New Testament, and were constantly quoting from the Epistle of Paul the Apostle to the Hebrews, ix., 22; "And almost all things are by the law purged with blood, and without shedding of blood is no remission;" and from the First Epistle of Paul to the Corinthians, v., 5; "To deliver such a one unto Satan for the destruction of the flesh, that the spirit may be saved in the day of the Lord Jesus." But Brigham Young and the modern Apostles preached in plainer language than Paul wrote; they proclaimed from the pulpit that you must kill the body to save the soul. So that every good (or bad) Mormon who attempted to forsake the faith and escape the country was mercilessly shot down. Some were assassinated for merely contemplating apostasy, the idea preached being that if they escaped the Lord Himself could not save them, but if their bodies were killed within the pale of (Zion) Salt Lake City they went straight to heaven.

An old farmer named William Parish, who with his two sons, Beason and Enoch, lived in the little walled town of Springville, south of Provo, was known to be on the verge of apostasy and to be making preparations to escape from the country. Just after dark one evening, as the old man and his two sons reached the wall of the town on their way home from the farm, they were fired upon and the old man and the elder son, Benson, fell dead, while Enoch leaped over the wall and broke his hip, so that he became a cripple for life. Enoch Parish, being a mere boy, was permitted to live, and after he had recovered so as to be able to limp about, by permission of Brigham Young he accompanied my party to San Bernardino, Cal., but returned to his vomit, as he was a good Mormon.

My particular chum and running mate in the city (Salt Lake) was a young man named Joe Hunt, son of old "Daddy Hunt," of San Bernardino, Cal., an enthusiastic old Mormon, whom I afterward met in San Bernardino, and who had been a member of the California Assembly. It was common report in Salt Lake City that Joe Hunt could not apostatize, or rather dare not leave Utah, as he had committed crimes both in Missouri and California, and dared not go either east or west. Therefore, he was a sort of privileged character and could say pretty much what he pleased about Mormonism without danger. He was neither a pious nor orthodox Mormon, he was too intelligent for that, and he criticized the dogmas of the church and the acts of the apostles without stint. One afternoon I met Joe Hunt up town when he asked me to come up after supper and accompany him to the Third ward school house where, he said, I could see a new phase of Mormonism. I thought he meant the palaver they called "speaking in tongues" when they reached the shouting stage of excitement, and at first I declined to go. But Joe declared the performance would be something else altogether, and that it would be something new and interesting to me. So I joined him that evening and when we reached the end door of the school house we saw a group of men and women circled about the front of the teacher's stand, singing, praying, hallelujahing and repeating from the Bible "there is more rejoicing in heaven over one sinner saved than over a thousand righteous brought to judgment." On approaching the crowd we saw within the circle, stripped to the waist and laid out on benches, the dead bodies of two fine looking, middle-aged men-one with eleven buckshot through the breast and the other with a bullet wound apparently through the heart. They had been Mormons, had apostatized and attempted to escape to the American army. They had been blood atoned, they had been "saved." And such incidents were of frequent occurrence in those days.

While I felt fairly secure myself, under such auspices as I enjoyed, I could not help but think upon what a slender thread hung the lives of the eight or ten suspicioned young Gentiles stopping at the Townsend House, when these blood-thirsty fanatics could sincerely rejoice over the assassination of men of their own faith, and were being daily taught that it was just as harmless and dutiful an act to kill a Gentile as to kill a venomous snake.

One morning I met Joe Hunt and he asked me if I had heard of the latest capture. I replied in the negative, when he said that six Californians, with a splendid and valuable outfit and $18,000 in gold coin, had been captured up at Ogden while attempting to cross over to the American army, and had been brought down to the city and were then at the Townsend House. We went down to the hotel, ascended to the second floor and went to the open door of a large room in front of which an armed Mormon sentinel was pacing. Here we found six large, intelligent, manly-looking American mountaineers, somewhat grizzled by age. This was the Aiken party, for the subsequent murder of whom Brigham Young was afterward indicted. The party consisted of John and Thomas Aiken (brothers) who had been old scouts and guides for the army in the Indian wars of early days in California; A. J. Jones, an old grizzly bear hunter in Mariposa County, Cal., where he was well known and universally esteemed as "Honesty Jones," and three others whose names I never learned or have entirely forgotten. We talked with them awhile, and they appeared cheerful and not to apprehend any danger and temporary detention. On going up town I asked Joe Hunt what they (the church authorities) would do with the men.

"Oh, they will turn them loose," he replied with a significant toss of the head.

"Will they let them go on to the army?" I enquired.

"No," promptly replied Hunt.

"Will they let them return to California?" I enquired.

"They will let them start back," replied Hunt, with a significant accent on the word "start".

"But will they get through?" was the next question.

"No," replied Hunt, with some deliberation.

"Why not?" I asked.

"Because they have too much valuable plunder," replied Hunt, with some nonchalance?

Hunt knew the Mormons better than I did. The Aiken party was afterward assassinated at the crossing of Sevier River, a short day's ride north of Fillmore City.

When Brigham Young decided to enter into open rebellion against the authority of the United States it was, by appointment, the legal Governor of the Territory of Utah. He ordered all Gentile Federal officers (including United States Judges) out of the Territory, and declared Martial Law, which placed everybody and everything within his jurisdiction under his personal dictatorship. To disobey was certain death. He ordered all Gentile members and employees of the American mercantile houses of Gilbert & Gerrish and Livingston, Kinkaed & Co., to either leave the territory or take their turn in the Mormon army. They decided to leave, Brigham Young taking over the remnant of their stocks of goods.

A man named Huntington, who then lived at Springville, and Horace Clark, who had a wife in nearly every town between Salt Lake City and San Bernardino (good and obedient Mormon), had been running the mail line to San Bernardino until the suspension of that service, which left on their hands a lot of idle mules and vehicles. From these they began to fit up some light spring wagons with covers and four-mule teams to take the merchants and clerks out of the country.

Myself and several other young Gentiles applied to Huntingdon & Clark for passage, and were told that the terms would be $100 cash in advance, each to care for and drive a team and furnish his own provisions and bedding. Five of us acceded to the terms to pay our own way, work our passage and pay our own board and lodging. Each man was also required to get a written passport from Brigham Young. My passport read as follows;

> "John I. Ginn, of Ackworth, Georgia, 'recently of the expedition against Utah,' is hereby permitted to pass peacefully through the Territory of Utah on his way to California.

"(Signed)" Brigham Young,
"Governor."

All of the passports were similar in reading, and these we had to have translated and read to five different tribes or bands of Indians.

Before leaving the city, however, I wish to relate one incident going to show the acute mental, as well as physical, suffering entailed by Mormonism. In company with a Gentile companion I was one day passing an isolated dwelling in the southeastern portion of the city when a modest and handsome young woman hailed us and walked out to the front gate to inquire if we had any washing or mending to be done, adding that she had to earn her own bread and was having a hard time of it. I was curious to know something of her history and inquired. She said she was not a Mormon, but was married to one; that she was born and reared in Manchester, England, where she was living happily with her two brothers (the only living relatives she had), who were brass finishers, superior workmen and commanded the highest wages, when the two brothers became converted to Mormonism through the efforts of a bishop missionary, and were finally persuaded that it was necessary to their salvation that they go to (Zion) Salt Lake City. They tried in vain to convert her, and finally told her that they felt impelled to go, and that she could either remain in Manchester alone or go to Zion with them.

They had always been kindly and affectionate brothers, and she could not bear the idea of parting, and so decided to go with them and share their fate, whatever it might be. The two brothers had saved up L800 sterling between them. In company with a number of other converts, all under the command of the bishop, they took a sailing vessel for New Orleans. On the voyage one of the brothers died, whereupon the bishop appropriated one half of the joint funds to the church. On the way out across the plains from the Missouri river the other brother died, when the bishop appropriated (to the church or to himself) the other L400 sterling, leaving the poor girl without a penny or a protector and she even had to beg very hard for an old waistcoat one of the brothers had worn, which she still preserved as a souvenir, and which she exhibited to us while the tears were streaming down her checks.

Arriving in Salt Lake City one afternoon the “herd” of immigrants were rounded up in front of the Tithing House, when one of the leading church dignitaries approached this heart-broken and defenseless girl and inquired who was her protector. She replied she had none, and explained the cause. The harsh-voiced brute replied; “Then you must get married.” The girl answered that she would do so as soon as she had time to look around and find a man to suit her. “You must get married right here and now,” retorted the brute. The girl said she then burst into tears, covered her face with one hand and with the other reached back until her hand came in contact with a man's shoulder when she replied; "Well, I will take this man," and they were married on the spot. She said he had proved to be a passably good sort of man; that he had several other wives scattered about the city, and he lived with these most of his time and seldom bothered her but she was enceinte. She inquired eagerly about the probability of the American army coming in, and on being told that it probably could not force a passage through the mountains before spring, she pointed to the east and exclaimed with great earnestness; "Oh, how I wish it would appear upon the slope tomorrow morning and shell the city, and that the first shell would explode between my feet and put an end to my miserable existence." A few other incidents of my stay in the city of the Saints might be cited to show the trend of thought among these religious fanatics after their reasoning faculties had become wholly subordinated to and subverted by their faith.

Being a printer myself and having served my apprenticeship in Montgomery, Ala. among a number of old New Orleans printers, soon after my arrival I became quite intimate with an old Crescent City, CA printer then employed on the Desert News, the chief organ of the Mormon Church. Through this source I found ready access to the back files of the paper, and I spent many days in the office reading them over.

In one number was a sermon delivered in the Tabernacle by Brighham Young just after he had heard of the Killing of Apostle Parley Parker Pratt by Hector McLean of San Francisco, near Fort Smith in the Indian Territory. Brigham wound up with the prophesy that "the Lord will avenge the death of His Apostle by the death of an hundred to one." Hence the massacre of 136 men, women and children at Mountain Meadows that same season. Brigham had the power in his own hands to fulfill that prophesy when he made it, and he fulfilled it relentlessly.

THE DAILY INDEPENDENT

Virginia City, Nevada Saturday, December 12, 1874

Brigham Young's Divorces Decided
By a Mormon Justice to be Valid.
Salt Lake, December 11.

A Mormon Justice of the Peace of this city, haves just decided in a civil action that divorces granted by Brigham Young are Valid. An appeal has been taken, with a view to expose and test the legality of the Mormon Church divorce system.

Many persons have been divorced by Brigham against their wishes, and they seek redress in the District Courts.

Author's collection.

Another number of the paper contained a speech delivered by Brigham at a gathering on Cottonwood Creek, a few miles southeast of the city, on the occasion of the celebration of the tenth anniversary of the arrival of the Saints in the valley. My memory is not clear on the date, but I think it was the 24th of July. In that speech he said that when he pitched his tent on that very spot in 1847 he prayed to the Lord to give the Saints ten years of peace, and had promised the Lord that if He would grant that petition he (Brigham) would so strengthen His chosen people that they would be able to defy not only the Gentiles of the United States, but of all the world combined. He thanked God that that prayer had been answered, and that now the saints could whip all the powers on the earth. And the people believed this bombast. It was physical and spiritual death to doubt the word of the Prophet.

My printer friend had taken a deep interest in my spiritual welfare, believing, as Mother Taylor did, that I was destined to become an earnest and enthusiastic Mormon, and when he learned that I had obtained a passport and had made arrangements to leave, he came at me with an earnest and eloquent appeal to desist from such a fatal step, assuring me that within the immediate future all the peoples on the earth, outside of Zion, were to perish miserably and utterly, some by earth quakes, some by famine and some by pestilence and some by plagues. I was charmed by his eloquence, impressed with his earnestness and amused at his credulity and hallucination. I listened to him silently for awhile and then, calling him by name, replied; "Supposing you were back in New Orleans in one of the large saloons where the old time printers used to assemble, and Ned Buntline (E.Z.C. Judson), Tom Ownby, Ed Knight and Ed Powers were seated about the round table with you and you should make that talk to them, what do you think they would say?" He reflected for a moment on the critical intelligence of his old time companions, burst into a hearty laugh and replied; "Well I expect it would appear foolish to them."

Mother Taylor also took a deep interest in my spiritual welfare and also laid siege to dissuade me from leaving, pointing out the perils of such a trip and expressing great fear that I might be killed by the Indians. I told her I had a passport from Brother Brigham, but she expressed fear that that might not save me. Then I put a poser to her;

"Mother Taylor, do you believe Brother Brigham would deliberately give me a passport, implying immunity from danger from both white and red Mormons, when he knew or believed I was at all likely to be killed by Indians?"

"No, I don't believe Brother Brigham would do that but then you might be killed on the road," and at that she dropped the subject. One day while I was sitting in my room at the head of the stairway, reading, a large, queenly-looking young woman came to visit Mother Taylor in the room below, from which, through an open stairway, I could hear every word spoken above a whisper.

"What do you think Mother Taylor; old Elder so-and-so wants me to marry him," opened the young woman, in a loud, shrill voice.

"Well, are you going to marry him?" inquired Mother Taylor, quietly.

"No, I am not," emphatically replied the visitor.

"But suppose he carries the matter before Brother Brigham, and Brother Brigham says it is necessary for the elder's soul's salvation that you marry him, what then?"

"His soul be damned," snapped the young queen;

"I'd see him and Brother Brigham both in hell before I would marry the old beast and go and live with his five or six other wives, one of them a squaw at that."

It is hardly necessary to add that Mother Taylor was distinctly shocked.

CHAPTER III

Through The Enemies Country.

Everything being in readiness, our party left Salt Lake city for San Bernardino, Cal., 600 miles, in five light spring wagons, well covered, and each drawn by four good mules. The party consisted of Wm. Huntington and wife of the firm of Livingston, Kinkaed & Co.; an Englishman and wife (name not remembered); myself, Ike Robbins, a harness maker from Texas; Jack Mendenhall of South Bend, Ind., who had been a clerk in one of the Gentile stores; Charley Ashton and John Garber (the latter a fancifully dressed bar-keeper) from Cincinnati, and a large young Virginia Irishman who went by the name Michael Virginia, all Gentiles; Huntington and Horace Clark owners of the outfit; Enoch Parish, and a short, stout, young English Mormon, all Mormons, and for guide and interpreter we had Jacob Hamblin, a Mormon cattleman, who had a ranch five miles north of the Mountain Meadows, and of whom I will have something further to say in connection with the atrocious massacre of emigrants at the Mountain Meadows.

Two other young Gentiles left the city a few days ahead of us on horseback, with the intention of riding down through the Mormon settlements as far as Cedar City (about halfway of the trip), and there resting up their animals, so that they would be able to keep up with the teams across the desert stretches beyond, where we would be traveling from 50 to 63 miles per day. When we reached Fillmore City, then the Mormon capital, we found both of them had been shot dead in the streets of that town by an Indian named, "Shot," brother to Kanosh, Chief of the Parovans or Pahvents.

The Aiken party of six Californians was released and left the city a day or two after we did, and pushed ahead rapidly to overtake us before we passed out of the settlements, so as to be our company through the Indian country. We reached the crossing of Sevier River, between the little town of Summit Creek, where we had stopped the night before, and Fillmore City, where we would stop the next night, and went into camp on the meadow on the south or left bank of the stream near sunset. Jake Hamblin evidently knew what was to take place at that point that night, as subsequent events proved. He asked us to gather a good supply of dry cottonwood limbs with which to build large fires after dark, and hurry up supper, saying that after dark we would hitch up and drive about three miles up the mountain and make a "still camp" in a cedar forest some distance off the road, leaving large fires burning at the crossing, which, he said, was a "bad place for Indians" and yet all the Indians in the territory at that time were as completely under the control of Brigham Young as were the white Mormons. We did as directed, however, gathered the wood, hurried through with supper, hitched up, piled the dry limbs upon the camp fires and drove off up the mountain. Half an hour afterward, as we learned next night through couriers, the Aiken party rode up to these fires, dismounted, and while they were unsaddling and unpacking their animals, five of them were shot dead and the sixth one mortally wounded.

The wounded man was taken back to Summit Creek by the assassins (Danites or Destroying Angels from Salt Lake City), where he lingered four or five days in great agony before death put an end to his sufferings. An intelligent young woman waited upon him tenderly until he died, and to her he related the full details of the killing.

When the federal army and judiciary got into the valley the following summer (1858) United States Judge Cradlebaugh instituted a searching inquiry into the Mountain Meadow Massacre and all other killings he could hear of as having occurred during the reign of terror the previous year. But all Mormons were profoundly silent about the assassination of the Aiken party.

On my arrival in California in the latter part of (1857) I reported both the Mountain Meadows and the Aiken massacres, and the accounts were published throughout the state, arousing great sympathy and the deepest indignation for the "Aiken boys" especially were well known and universally esteemed. On taking up my residence in Mariposa County, CA that winter Miles Goodman, a prominent man of the county and lifelong and intimate friend of Honesty Jones (one of the Aiken party), and who had known both Jones and the latter's wife back in Pennsylvania, having read the account of the killing, came to me for further details. I told him the story as it had overtaken me on the road in some mysterious way, and he wrote to Mrs. Jones. In the spring of 1858 Mrs. Jones wrote Goodman to try to furnish her with sufficient legal evidence of the death of her husband as to enable her to settle up his estate, as he was a man of some property. Goodman came to me and I wrote a letter of inquiry to Kirk Anderson, whom I had known in St. Louis as city editor of the Missouri Republican, and who had entered Salt Lake City with the army and started a red hot Gentile paper called the Valley Tan. Anderson published my letter in full, without comment, and it was like a clap of thunder in a clear sky, for not an officer, military or judicial, nor any other Gentile in Utah, had ever heard a whisper of the cold-blooded assassinations of the Aiken party solely for their valuables. Judge Cradlebaugh at once instituted an inquiry into the case, when the Summit Creek young woman who had nursed the wounded survivor of the party until his death, went into court and under oath related the story of the wounded man, which account of the affair was substantially as I had heard it the next night after the killing. Thus, Mrs. Jones got her legal evidence. I heard long afterward that Brigham Young was indicted for this sextuple murder-but that was the end of the affair.

Leaving our "still camp" in the cedar forest the next morning after the killing, we came to and stopped fifteen minutes at noon at a Mormon ranch or roadhouse about twelve miles short of Fillmore City.

A tall, blanketed Indian at the place scrutinized us closely for a few minutes and then struck off in a long trot through low brush toward a sugar-loaf peak rising 500 or 600 feet above the plain or valley four miles to the southwest. We started immediately and drove rapidly down grade over a smooth, hard road, but before we reached the stream on the northern border of Fillmore City we could see his signal smokes rising from the peak to notify the Parovan Indians on Corn Creek, eight miles beyond and south of Fillmore, that we were coming.

As we ascended the slope into the town the first sight that caught our eyes was the Indian, Shot, standing in the middle of the main street, facing us, and wearing a flashy red waistcoat belonging to one of the young Americans he had killed in the streets of the town a few days before. The Mormon at whose house we stopped that night told us Shot would not allow the whites to bury the murdered men for a day or two, but they had finally persuaded him to allow them to give the young men “a Christian” burial.

Shot inspected our whole outfit closely and then struck off for Corn Creek. The Parovans numbered about 400 men, all well armed, nearly every man having a gun of some sort and were, therefore, by odds the most formidable tribe in the whole territory, and the white Mormons told us we were likely to have trouble in trying to pass them. But the Parovans were good Mormons, their chief, Kanosh, being an elder in the Mormon Church and an intimate friend and most obedient servant of Brigham Young. The secret of this was that Kanosh had become smitten with one of Brigham’s concubines (some said the queenly looking Mrs. Eleanor McLean, whose first and second missteps paved the way for the Mountain Meadows Massacre), and Brigham had implied a promise to give her to him “some day” if he would be a good Indian and implicitly obey all orders. So Jake Hamblin, our guide and interpreter, engaged the grown up son of the Bishop of Fillmore and dispatched him to Corn Creek after Kanosh.

Kanosh mounted his horse at once and came up, leaving the tribe under the command of his brother, Shot, with strict orders to kill us if we attempted to pass before he returned in safety. Our passports were translated and read to Kanosh, who replied that we were alright; that whomsoever “Brother Brigham passed could go through without molestation.” We then engaged Kanosh and the Bishop’s son to go through with us to the next village, Red Creek, two days drive, we were to pay them each $25 per day. As we were descending a long gentle grassy slope toward the sink of Corn Creek next morning, we could see the Indians, mounted and on foot, dashing in squads from clump to clump of willows, working their way down to the road to intercept us. Their villages and farms were two or three miles to the east, up near the western base of the Wasatch Range of mountains. The stream, coming out of a deep gorge in the high range above, ran nearly due west until it came within about 100 yards of the road and then turned south, nearly parallel with the road for about 200 yards and then sank, leaving the road to pass below across a smooth, grassy valley or plain.

Kanosh, on horseback, rode on the opposite side of my covered ambulance, keeping concealed from view to test the fidelity of his brother and the tribe. Nearly all of the dismounted Indians, about 270 in number, had reached the willow jungle parallel and close to the road, while about 130 on horseback had assembled in a dense willow copse some 500 yards up the creek. When we had reached a point about opposite this mounted group they suddenly poured out in a swarm and, forming in double rank, about sixty-five abreast, they threw their bodies flat upon or down beside their horse's necks and charged upon us at a furious pace. Kanosh ordered us to halt and, dashing around in front of my team, he rode full speed toward the charging column. When within about fifty yards of them he halted, threw up both hands and called them to halt. Addressing a few words to them he wheeled and rode at full speed along the willows parallel to the road, addressing the footmen as he went, while the mounted men rode slowly down to within fifteen steps of us and drew up in line. Directly the footmen began to emerge from the willows and approach, assembling on the left flank to the south of the horsemen.

Directly Kanosh returned and, reining up his horse in front of the assembled warriors, he delivered a brief speech telling them that Brother Brigham had given us permission to pass, and that that settled it, but that the Gentiles might give them a few presents to remunerate them for their trouble. At this there was a very distinct murmur of disapproval. An old patriarch of the tribe named Parashont, sitting upon his horse, made an impassioned appeal to kill us anyway and take all we had and no thanks to us for presents. This put Kanosh upon his dignity and his metal, and he then called for a division of the tribe to see how many would obey his orders and how many those of Parashont. About two thirds drew over to the side of Kanosh and the other third drew up in line with Parashont, and the two leaders and their followers stood glaring at each other at a distance of about twelve paces. Kanosh ordered us to get every weapon ready for instant use, and to pour a deadly volley into the Parashont party the moment the ball opened. We had 96 ready shots without stopping to load and plenty of fixed ammunition. Then Kanosh made another speech to Parashont and his followers, telling them this was to be a fight to extermination; that if his side and the Gentiles won the fight not a single man of the opposition would be allowed to leave the ground alive.

That practically settled the affair; all but about twenty of Parashont's followers deserting him and going over to the side of Kanosh. The garrulous old Parashont, however, had to have the last word, remarking that he could follow and kill us himself, as he had fourteen grown sons in the party, whereupon Kanosh ordered his brother, Shot, to take command during his absence, with strict instructions to shoot any or all Indians who should attempt to leave camp before he returned. Shot was a savage proper, and Parashont knew it and, therefore, he said no more nor did he make any attempt to follow us. After distributing a few presents among them we drove on and, after a hard day's drive, camped at dark at a spring in a cedar forest a short distance from the road. Kanosh, being a Mormon elder, we had to have prayer in camp night and morning.

At midnight or later we heard a distant call and Kanosh walked out to answer it. The call was a runner sent out by Shot. Before we left Salt Lake City I had frequent conversations with a good-looking small young man with a handsome young wife. They had been Mormons and he was extremely anxious to get away with us, but was financially unable to do so. After we left it seems he procured an old buggy and team and himself and wife had started out expecting to overtake us, had reached Corn Creek the same day we passed there and had been detained by Shot, who dispatched a courier after Kanosh to know if he should let them pass. Kanosh simply told the courier; "Tell Shot to obey orders," and we never heard of the young man or his wife afterward.

And, by the way, I never heard of my fellow prisoner Joe Franks, after I left him in the city.

The next day we drove on to Red Creek, where we stopped for the night, and where Kanosh and the bishop's son turned back while we drove to Cedar City, where we remained two nights and one day at the house of bishop John D. Lee who, several years afterward, was tried, convicted and shot for his participation as commander of the Mormon militia in the Mountain Meadows Massacre.

Fearing the wrath to come, the Mormons everywhere, from one end of the territory to the other, had begun soon after the massacre, to formulate stories shifting the blame for that atrocious crime from their own to the shoulders of the Indians. But their stories were not consistent. At Salt Lake and all down the line to Fillmore City, about 140 miles, the story was that the Parovan Indians had followed and killed the emigrants because the latter had poisoned a spring near Corn Creek, causing the death of several of the Parovans and some of their cattle to die. But at Fillmore City and among the Parovans the story was altogether different, and was to the effect that "the Piutes south of the Rim of the Basin had killed them." South of the Rim or divide upon which the massacre took place the Santa Clara and Rio Virgin Indians had no hesitation in stating that the Mormons both planned and executed the tragedy, at the same time freely admitting that some of their own bands participated, by invitation, and for the little assistance they rendered they got a little flour and some remnants of clothing stripped from the bodies of the dead.

The Mormons had saved seventeen little children from the massacre, ten girls and seven boys, little tots, "such as are too young to tell tales," as Major Lee said to the council of war the night before the killing, when he said to the council; "It is ordered from headquarters that this party be used up." Bishop Major Lee pointed out to us two of these little tots, whom he had made full orphans, in his own house, and the next day a Mormon blacksmith to whom I had taken a wagon for repairs, pointed out three others, two girls and a boy, whom he had taken into his family. The others had been scattered about among other Mormons of Cedar City, Parovan and Harmony.

Leaving Cedar City we drove southwest to Pinto Creek, 24 miles, and 15 miles short of the scene of the massacre, where we stopped over another day, to enable Jake Hamblin, our guide and interpreter, to proceed over the Santa Clara and engage old Tutsegovet, big Chief over all the tribes south of the Rim of the Great Interior Basin, to come up, meet and travel with us through all the bands or tribes southwest to the Muddy River, 180 miles.

The first night we camped at the Pinto Creek springs a small and elderly Englishman came into our camp with a bundle containing two or three shirts and about three days provisions, carried on a stick over his shoulder. He was a Mormon fleeing from the reign of terror. We tried to dissuade him from proceeding next morning on foot, telling him we had plenty of provisions and would take him on to California in our wagons, but he was terror stricken, afraid he would be pursued and "blood-atoned." He was too small and too old to perform duty as a soldier, and therefore we did not think there was any danger of pursuit. We told him the southern Piutes would strip him, take his provisions and let him perish on the deserts ahead. He replied; "Oh, no; the poor things will not disturb a poor old man like me," and struck out.

Three days afterward, while passing through a lava bed on the Santa Clara River we came upon a band of Indians and among them stood the old Englishman, hungry, barefooted, bareheaded and with not a strip of clothing upon him except an old hickory shirt, scarcely reaching down to his hips. We picked him up, clothed him and carried him on till one night when we were making a long and rapid drive across a desert to reach the sink of the Mojave River, when he got out of one of the wagons, let those behind pass him and we never heard of him again.

Mormon Gunfighters

[The Territory of Utah had a number of deadly gunfighters within its boundaries. Among them, and probably the most notorious, were three men who had military backgrounds, having served in the Nauvoo Legion. They were William "Bill" Hickman, Lot Smith and Porter Rockwell. William "Bill" Hickman was a member of the Nauvoo Legion and served as a Captain of a Ranger Company consisting of 100 men, a guerilla force harassing military columns and supply lines of eight companies of the United States 10th Infantry during the "Mormon War." He was a practicing attorney in Utah Territory, was Sheriff of Green River, County and served as a U. S. Deputy Marshal for a short time. He also became an outlaw. He was considered an excellent shot with pistol or rifle. He died at Lander, Wyoming, August 21st, 1883, from an old bullet wound suffered in a gunfight with Lot Huntington on December 25th, 1859, on Main Street in Salt Lake City…thus depriving the army of about 500,000 pounds of provisions intended for its maintenance during the long and severe winter setting in. Twenty-years later, Porter Rockwell was indicted on two-counts of first-degree murder in the deaths of John and William Aiken.]

CHAPTER IV

The Mountain Meadows Massacre.

Early the second morning we drove to Mountain Meadows, the scene of the horrible butchery about three weeks prior to our arrival. The meadows being five miles north of the southern rim of the great interior basin and continue in a broad belt five miles southward to a point a few hundred yards south of the smooth, ovate summit where they terminate in marshy ground around a spring of fine water. Here, Jack Hamblin had told them, would be the best place for them to stop and let their livestock recuperate before starting out on the deserts beyond.

The emigrants had corralled their wagons a few steps west of the road and about thirty yards north of the spring, on dry ground. Here they were attacked by Indians and held until Major John D. Lee could assemble the Mormon Militia and get them upon the ground. As soon as they were attacked the emigrants dug an entrenchment around inside of their corral, throwing the earth from the ditch up under the wagons to form breast works. Inside of this enclosure the ground was matted with arrows which had been fired by the Indians, and all of which had been broken by the besieged just back of the iron or flint points, so that they could not again be used. This enclosure was also covered with both written and printed-paper torn into the finest fragments, apparently to destroy evidence of the identity of the party. This had undoubtedly been done by the Mormons after the surrender and slaughter. Nor was there a single dead body inside the corral. At the spring and along the trail leading down from the corral were four bodies, one man, one woman and two little girls, doubtless killed while attempting to get water.

A tall, black Indian named Jackson, and an honest sort of savage, who as chief of the Santa Clara band, was detailed by Tutsegovet to accompany my party as far as the Muddy in the capacity of Big Chief, afterward told Gen. J. H. Carleton, who was sent to the Meadows in May 1859, to "bury the bones of the victims of that terrible massacre," that Bishop John D. Lee, Isaac C. Haight, a prominent

Mormon of Cedar City, and sixty Mormon followers, all painted and disguised as Indians, joined in the siege, which lasted several days.

On the fifth day (according to the best authority I could find), finding the emigrants, who had 65 men and boys capable of good fighting, "fought like lions," as the Mormons expressed it, John D. Lee, Isaac C. Haight and John M. Higby, having removed their disguise and that of their Mormon militia, entered the emigrant camp under a flag of truce to negotiate for its surrender. Most of the livestock of the emigrants had already been killed or run off and these three treacherous fiends appealed to the emigrants to surrender their arms to them "as fellow Americans and fellow Christians," stating the surrender of their arms would appease the Indians and that they (the Mormons) would use their militia to guard the besieged people in safety back to Cedar City, where they would be free from molestation.

Finding themselves in a most perilous situation these people surrendered their arms to their own country-men. It was a fatal step, for they knew not the fierce and fiendish nature of the religious fanatics upon whose mercy they had thrown themselves.

The emigrants were then drawn up in a line, two abreast, with here and there a little child on the side led by its mother, and on each side of each couple marched an armed Mormon guard. In this order they took the road back toward Cedar City, and on going about one mile, over the summit and down the gentle slope, John M. Higby gave the signal for the slaughter and a fusillade was opened upon these defenseless people so treacherously disarmed, and 45 or 48 men, women and children clustered together, were shot down upon such a limited space that they fell across each other.

Then a halt was called, or rather the firing ceased, because the militia revolted at the sight, especially of the slaughter of women and children, as explained to me by a young Mormon in eastern Nevada years afterward, he saying he was present as a boy at the massacre. The march was then resumed and kept up for about another mile, toward Cedar City, when the conclusion was arrived at, after a general consultation, that it would not do to let the other adults escape to tell what had already been done, and the remainder of the emigrants were shot down in a huddle, all except seventeen small children, ten girls and seven boys," too young to tell tales," one of these, however, a little runt of a girl, proved to be twelve years of age and very bright, and afterward gave United Sates Judge Cradlebaugh a thrilling description of the massacres.

When we passed over the grounds, about three weeks after the slaughter, the bodies were still well preserved and most of them lay just as they had fallen, each wound that had caused death being immediately over the corresponding pool of coagulated blood on the ground. The eyes of all who had fallen upon side or back had been picked out by the crows, but otherwise none of the bodies had been mutilated nor disfigured by decay, the weather being cold, with a few patches of snow on the ground.

At the scene of the first slaughter one group of bodies presented a most pathetic picture. An old, white-haired man with a bullet hole through his temples lay on his left side with his legs partially drawn up. His right hand was clasped in the left hand of a tall handsome woman of perhaps 24 years. She had a head of very heavy, long, black hair, which lay upon the old man's knee, and the assassin's bullet had passed through her chest from side to side, probably through the heart. The woman's right hand clasped the left of a beautiful little girl of four or five years, whose skull had been crushed in in a long line above the right ear, as if by a rifle barrel. Her long white hair, matted with blood and brains, fell over the woman like a shroud, as the little one lay with her head upon the (perhaps mother's) hip. I took them to be father, daughter and granddaughter.

At this point a pit had been dug and a number of bodies thrown into it, but as it had not been covered over the wolves had pulled some of the bodies from the surface, and in doing so had mutilated them to some extent. Most of the bodies in this group, however, were still lying just as they fell, many of them (especially the men) having been stripped of clothing by the Indians after the Mormons had killed them.

That these people, nominally Christians, free from guilt or any crime against the Mormons or any other sect, were slaughtered by the Mormons, for Christ's sake, there is no room for doubt. All of them, except a few women and girls who had their throats cut, were killed by bullet wounds, and yet there were but three old guns among all of the Indians who could possibly have assisted in the slaughter. I passed through all of the Indians south of the rim of the basin soon afterward, those of Santa Clare, the Rio Virgin, the Muddy and the Vegas, and saw but three guns among them. The Mormons got all the plunder of the train, the Indians but little clothing even. The money of the party, the horses, mules, cattle, wagons, family carriages, household goods, and even much of the bloody clothing stripped from the bodies of the murdered people, were taken to the Mormon Tithing House (an official building) in Cedar City, and there disposed of by the Mormon officials for the benefit of the Mormon church.

General Carleton, in his official report on the affair, made nearly two years afterward, picturing the march of these people from the camp to the points where they were to be mercilessly shot down, says; "It brings to the mind a picture of human suffering and wretchedness on the one hand, and of human treachery and ferocity on the other, that cannot possibly be excelled by any other scene that ever before occurred in real life." In another paragraph he speaks of "this crime that for hellish atrocity has no parallel in our history." Certainly no such savage, heartless, inexcusable, treacherous and atrocious massacre was ever committed by Indians on this continent not even those in the Wyoming Valley in Pennsylvania nor that of Fort Mimms in Alabama, and I can recall but two in all history that approach it in atrocity. Each of them, like this, a religious massacre; that of the Albigeneses at Beziers, France, in1207, when, under a crusade proclaimed against them by Pope Innocent III., the entire population, Catholics as well as heretics, were put to death, Arnold, the Pope's legate, saying; "Kill them all God will find His own;" and the other was the massacre of St. Bartholomew, August 24th, 1572, when 70,000 Huguenots or French Protestants were shot to death in the streets of Paris by their neighbors.

The people thus so cruelly murdered were well-to-do people from Arkansas and Northeastern Texas, and were known as the "Perkins Party" or the "Fancher Party," a man named Perkins, who had been to California before, being in charge of the train. They had about forty wagons, with forty families (about 137 persons in all), a family physician, fine stock, three fine family carriages and doubtless large sums of money. They were well dressed, quiet, orderly and genteel, and doubtless constituted the wealthiest train that ever crossed the plains.

Another strong Texas train, composed of a large number of experienced and fearless Indian fighters, was making forced marches southward from Salt Lake City to overtake the Perkins Party (or Francher party) before they reached the Indian country proper, and on the very day the Perkins party was being slaughtered, Jake Hamblin, as guide, took the Texas party across the summit, four miles east of the Meadows, where they had to let their wagons down the mountain by ropes. This I learned from the Texas party upon my arrival in San Bernardino, and told them of the massacre. Yet Jake Hamblin, in his story to General Carleton whitewashing the Mormons, said he was "up north," or about Fillmore City, at the time of the massacre, and hurried southward afterward when he heard the Indians were about to attack the Texas party. To save himself and his fellow Mormons from the results of an investigation; Hamblin had also previously told the same false story to Judge Cradlebaugh.

The seventeen little children spared from the massacre were distributed among the Mormons of Cedar City and other southern settlements, and were afterward gathered up by Dr. Forney, a Government Agent, and restored to their relatives in Arkansas. About 1898 I read an account of a reunion in Arkansas of the survivors of this horrible butchery most of whom were then men and women past middle age, and with large families of children of their own. When Dr. Forney went to gather up these children, the Mormon murderers of their parents and protectors claimed from $200 to $400 per head for the cost of keeping them.

THE SAN FRANSCIO CHRONICLE, CAILF.

September, 17th 1876

MOUNTAIN MEADOWS.

The Mormon murderer, John D. Lee,
Again on Trial.

Horrible Disclosures of the Atrocities
Committed on the Emigrants-A
Weak Prosecution.

{Special Dispatch to the Chronicle.}

Salt Lake, September16.-In the Beaver Court this Morning Jacob Hamblin in his testimony stated that John D. Lee told him that an Indian chief who lived at Cedar brought two girls who had been hiding in the brush to him (Lee) and asked what he should do with them-that they were too pretty to kill. Lee replied that he must shoot them: that they were too big.

The Indian then shot one and Lee threw the other down and cut her throat. That when Hamblin returned to his ranch he went over the ground and found the bodies of two girls about the ages described (from 13 to 15), lying near together with their throats cut, as described to him by another of the children who was about 8 years old and was at his house, and who claimed the two bodies as her sisters, and that their name was Dunlap. Hamblin, on being asked by the defense if he had ever told this to any one, replied that he had, and more too: that soon, after the occurrence, when he remember it better than he did now, he had told it to President Young and George A. Smith. That

President Young told him that when the right time came and we could get a court of justice to go and tell it, and on being further pressed, said he had not seen the effects of any court of justice from that time to this, but thought now was just the right time to till it.

Johnson, on being recalled. Stated that subsequent to the massacre he was sent to protect the next company of emigrants to the Santa Clara; that on his way he stopped at Harmony, where he saw John D. Lee, who proposed to him to get the emigrants into an ambush to destroy them by the Indians, and so get their property; also that he (Johnson) replied: "There has been too much bloodshed by you already. I have been instructed to see them safely through, and I will do so or die with them." That Lee then abused him, calling him ugly names. That he identified the prisoner at the bar as being John D. Lee.

The prosecution rested their case here, to the surprise of all in Court.

Lee's attorney announced that they also rested their case, and would not introduce any witnesses, but give the case to the jury on the evidence already adduced by the prosecution, and asked for a continuance until Monday, the 18th, to give them time to prepare the argument and instructions to the jury.

The Court adjourned till Monday at 10 o'clock, and instructed the witnesses to remain, as other cases pertaining to the massacre were to be disposed of.

The following documentary evidence has been filed by the prosecution, but was not given to the jury: A letter from John D. Lee to Brigham Young, dated November 20th, 1857, giving a report of the massacre as an Indian affair; a letter from Brigham Young to J. W. Denver, Commissioner of Indian Affairs, dated September 12th, 1857; a letter from the same to the same, January 6th, 1858; the proclamation of Governor Young, September 15th, 1857; affidavits of Brigham

Young and George A. Smith, July 30th, 1857; and a letter from Brigham Young to Bishop Dame, September 14th, 1857.

From-Dennis Fancher, of NY.
A distant relative of,
Captain Alexander Fancher.

A word as to the primary cause of the prophecy and its fulfillment of this most treacherous and atrocious slaughter; In 1855-6 the Mormons had a church in San Francisco and published a weekly paper there called the 'Wide West'. An active and thorough business-man named Hector McLean, who was then agent in that city for the Pacific Mail (Panama) Steamship Company, had a tall handsome wife and two beautiful little daughters. Under the ministrations of Apostle Parley Parker Pratt, Mrs. Eleanor Mclean[##] became converted to Mormonism, became completely daft on the subject. She tried in vain to convert her husband, and at length told him she felt that her soul's salvation depended upon her compliance with the decree of Brother Brigham, that all the faithful must go to (Zion) Salt Lake City. Mr. McLean told her that if she had become crazy enough for that, to go, and that he would take his two little girls to New Orleans and place them with her mother, to be properly reared and educated, which he did. Mrs. Mclean went to Zion with Apostle Pratt.

Some time afterward Mclean had occasion to make a hurried business visit to New York by steamer, and not having time to call by New Orleans to see his children, he telegraphed his mother-in-law from New York to know how they were. The old lady telegraphed that his wife had been there, kidnapped the children and disappeared.

At this McLean dropped all business, telegraphed Captain Cuzzens, a famous detective of St. Louis, to join him and started for New Orleans. Arriving there he learned that his ex-wife had gone to her mother, falling upon her knees, said that she felt that Mr. McLean would never speak to her again, but that she had repented of her folly and could not bear to be away from her children, and begged her mother, tears in her eyes, to allow her to remain at the old home. Of coarse the mother received the prodigal with open arms. Shortly afterward the saintly Pratt registered at one of the Crescent City Hotels, and a day or two later the Apostle, the weak-minded woman and the two little girls disappeared. McLean and Cozzens took up the trail, chased the fugitives up the Mississippi and Ohio rivers as far as

[##] Mrs. McLean, Born in Port Gibson, Mississippi, her parents removed to New Orleans, where her father through his invention of the cotton tie, became wealthy prior to his death.

Cincinnati, thence down again via New Orleans, up Red River and to a point in Texas, where they learned Pratt, with the woman and children, had fitted out a train of proselytes and gone up through the Indian Territory to take the northern road to Salt Lake City.

McLean then dismissed Captain Cozzens, returned up the Mississippi and struck out to Fort Smith to intercept the train. Arriving at a military post, under command of an Army Captain, in the Indian Territory, he told his story and asked to swear out a warrant against Pratt for kidnapping the children. The Captain replied that he had no jurisdiction in civil law, but added that under the circumstances he would use sufficient force to rescue the children.

At length the train arrived and McLean demanded his children, which were readily given up. The Mormon train proceeded on two or three miles to a stream and went into camp for the night. That evening, though happy in the possession of his precious little ones, McLean was beside himself with rage. He felt that he had been deeply wronged, put to much trouble, anxiety and expense, and ought to have some sort of satisfaction. He asked the officer for a warrant for the arrest of Pratt on a charge of petty larceny in stealing the clothing on the little girls. The Captain gave about the same reply as before, and went to bed.

McLean paced the barracks until after mid-night, and then asked a sentinel to awaken the Captain. On being awakened the officer invited his guest to enter, when McLean inquired in an earnest tone;

"Have you got a swift, sure-footed horse."

"The best in the territory," replied the officer.

"And a sure-fire rifle that will shoot where you hold it?" asked McLean.

"The best ever mad," said the Captain.

"Will you lend them to me?"

"I will," replied the officer, and ordered the horse brought out and saddled and the rifle carefully cleaned and freshly loaded.

Hector McLean took the rifle, mounted the horse and rode off just before daylight in the direction the Mormon train had taken.

Apostle Pratt evidently feared that he was not to get off so easily, as when McLean reached the camp, just after daylight, the Moron teams had already been hitched up and the wagons stretched out on the road ready to start. Pratt was standing out to one side when McLean rode up to within twenty steps of him, raised the rifle, took deliberate aim and shot him dead. Without a word he then wheeled the horse about, rode back to the post, delivered up the horse and gun and told the officer what he had done. The Captain replied coolly;

"Now, take your children back to their grandmother," which he did, and then returned to San Francisco.

Mrs. Eleanor McLean continued with the train to Salt Lake City, where she made her home with Brigham Young and his numerous other concubines in the Lion Mansion, and where she was frequently pointed out to me by Mormons on the street during my sojourn in the city of the saints.

Soon after the arrival of this train, with the first news of the tragic death of Parley Parker Pratt, Brigham Young uttered the "prophecy" in the Tabernacle that "the Lord will avenge the death of His Apostle by the death of an hundred to one" and he was careful to pick out doubtless the wealthiest party of emigrants who ever crossed the plains upon whom to wreck his vengeance and gratify his avarice by the fulfillment of this prophecy.

Taking into consideration all the precedent as well as subsequent facts bearing upon this awful slaughter of 136 innocent and treacherously disarmed men, women and children, the bullet wounds and the gun-less condition of the Indians, and all the environments of the tragedy, there is no foundation whatever on which to base the shadow of a doubt that the Mormons perpetrated the awful crime, and that they committed it with the knowledge and consent and by the order of the highest authorities of the Mormon Church. Chief Jackson of the Santa Clara Indians told General Carleton that Brigham Young sent him a letter ordering the killing of these emigrants, and Chief Touche of the Rio Virgin bands told the same officer that Brigham Young sent him a letter to the same effect, the letter being conveyed to him by Huntington, the man who furnished my party with transportation and accompanied us to California.

What I have written on this and other matters that came under my observation during the tragic year of 1857 has not been shaded by any prejudice I have against the Mormon religion, nor by any bias I might feel in favor of any other form of irrational superstition.

Jake Hamblin's own Indian, Albert, who accompanied us on horseback, could not bear to view the shocking sight again, but left us before we reached the most northerly group of dead bodies and rode around the place, through the brush and over the hills, far out to the eastward, returning to the road and rejoining us down on the Santa Clara, two miles south from the fatal camp at the meadow spring.

Following the little beaten path from where the emigrants had fortified their corral down toward the spring, I saw a piece of barrel stave sloping down in the mud under a turf of grass, a few steps east of the trail. Thinking this might conceal some statement or document I stepped out to it and raised the stave up. Beneath it I found three or four leaves of a printed pamphlet pertaining to a certain Masonic lodge in Texas. On the last page was a long printed list of names of members. This was the only scrap of paper larger than a child's fingernail I found upon the premises. This I carefully preserved and carried on to Los Angeles, where I gave it to Major Ben Trueman, who was then publishing a weekly newspaper in that village. Major Trueman told me he was a Mason and would write to the lodge named in the pamphlet and institute inquiry as to the identity of the murdered people. This he did, and the inquiry thus started in Northern Texas and in Arkansas, soon brought out a full knowledge of who the murdered people were, and afterward enabled Dr. Forney to find the relatives and friends of the Mountain Meadows orphans, and to whom the little ones were delivered.

CHAPTER V

Among The Arizona Indians

Leaving the scene of the massacre about noon, we plunged down the mountain southward into the canyon of the Santa Clara River. Reaching the stream in a forest of Aspen trees and brush, we ran into a band of forty or fifty Indians. These were the nearest Indians to the scene of the massacre, and they were fairly well togged out in the second hand clothing of the murdered emigrants. I had seen Indians in picturesque garb before, but the most pompous, gorgeous and picturesque individual I ever saw was a tall, black buck of middle age in this band. On his head he wore an antiquated but unusually tall bell crown silk hat, jauntily tipped to one side. On his body he wore a fiery red flannel shirt of ample proportion and over this, buttoned up to the throat, an old-fashioned claw-hammer coat of blue broadcloth and brilliant brass buttons but in order the better to display the dazzling rear tail of his bright red shirt, he had cut off the tails of the coat close up to the waist. Under or below these he wore nothing but a greasy old breech-cloth.

Pushing forward rapidly we passed through several small bands of Indians during the afternoon, all of whom fell into the road behind us and followed in a long trot, so that when we went into camp at the base of a steep little hill at dusk we had about 150 Piutes with us. The five wagons were drawn up side by side, a few steps apart, the mules turned out to graze, and all the men struck out for the flat near the river to gather firewood. The merchant party got back first, started their camp-fire in the rear of the upper wagon, and the two women were cooking when we returned. One of the men was a few steps ahead of me when I called to him to throw his wood in front of our wagon, so that we could watch the front and only open part of the wagons, "as these Indians will steal." Some of the Indians understood this reflection on their honesty and began to mutter and withdraw from the camp. Forming into a semi-circle a few steps up the side of the steep hill, they kept jabbering in angry tones, growing louder and louder, and every time I would show up in the light of the camp fire they would point their fingers at me as one man and in a loud and angry tone repeat the word "Steal; Steal."

It was now quite dark and things looked squally, with 150 Indians at close range constantly fanning the flame of their own and one another's anger, for you can scarcely run a hungry Indian out of camp at meal time, even with a gun. Directly Big Chief Tutsegovet rode up on the opposite side of our camp and stopped his pony out in the dark (with Jake Hamblin at his heels) to get the drift of the angry and threatening words of the Indians upon the hillside. After listening to them for a while he rode up to my camp fire and dismounted. He then called the Indians down from the hillside, gave them a severe lecture and ordered the last one of them to leave camp, telling them that because of their bad behavior he would not allow us to give them a bite to eat either that night or next morning. Among other things said, he opened with; "You are working yourselves up into a high state of excitement and deep indignation because some one of these people said you would steal, when you know you will steal everything you can get your hands upon, whether it is of any use to you or not; you would steal an old wagon hub with all the spokes broken off in it, even where there was plenty of dry wood lying around."

In spite of this lecture, however, some of them slipped into camp that night and cut off the rear end of my wagon cover, while I was asleep in the wagon. The next morning Tutsegovet announced that he was asleep in the wagon. The next morning on Tutsegovet announced that he was physically unable to accompany us as far as the Muddy, about three days' ride but detailed Chief Jackson of the Santa Clara to go with us, with all the authority of Big Chief. Jackson was fond of exercising his authority as Big Chief, and made the Rio Virgin bands toe the mark, ordering one band, under penalty of death, to return an old table knife they had stolen from the women's mess. The knife was promptly returned.

One day we crossed over a very high mountain from the Rio Virgin to the Muddy. Fortunately, as subsequent events proved, Jake Hamblin drove on some hours ahead of us in his buggy. There were 500 warriors at the Muddy, and as they knew of our coming they had made every preparation to kill us before we reached the ford. This tribe had two chiefs, Isaac and Thomas, of apparently equal authority, and two Mormon missionaries were stopping there to instruct them in Mormonism and agriculture. The whole tribe, armed with buck-horn bows and arrows (with which they could shoot sixty yards with great accuracy and deadly effect), had been distributed for a mile or more along the roadside concealed in a jungle of tulles and willows. Hamblin had reached there in time, explained matters to Isaac and Thomas, and they decided to let us pass, sending out runners to call the Indians in from their ambuscade. As we descended the mountain overlooking the valley we could see the runners darting from place to place through the tulles, and every now and then a band of 40 or 50 Indians would rise up, strike the road and proceed on to the ford, to which we drove and encamped until the next afternoon.

The Muddy is a warm stream or creek of considerable volume, coming from hot springs a few miles west of the road, and in the valley between the road and these springs the Indians were farming. During the early hours, at least of that evening, all of the 500 bucks and many of their squaws remained in camp with us. We fed them well, and then got them to sing and dance for us. They sang well, one love-song, in particular, having a plaintive and beautiful air, while the words were touching and romantic. The refrain was "El Llano Estakado" (The Staked Plains) Llano, the Spanish for plains, being pronounced Yano) and the story was of a lovely Piute girl having been stolen by Comanche Indians and spirited away to the Staked Plains of Texas; her Piute lover gave pursuit, he in turn being followed by a band of his tribesmen to save him from harm. The intrepid lover finally crept into the Comanche camp at night, rescued his sweetheart and started back to his own country. The Comanches in turn gave pursuit, and just as they were about to overtake him he met his tribesmen coming to his rescue. They turned upon the Comanches and slaughtered them, the young lover performing prodigious deeds of valor, and then the whole party returned to their own country in safety, where the young lovers were "married and lived happy ever after".

Their dances with accompanying low chant in monotone harmony, as the whole circle around the camp fire, with a loud grunt in unison, with arms locked, leap simultaneously into the air and every foot comes down heavily upon the ground at the same instant, are weird and almost demonical. They enjoy these dances, or circular sidewise jumps, and will keep them up for an hour at a time and look pleasant. But some one of our party that evening (I think it was one of the woman) made the mistake of getting them to give an exhibition of a war dance. They started in, and in a few minutes they became wild and intensely excited, as if under the influence of strong drink, and began to cast sinister and vicious glances at the Gentile bystanders, when Jake Hamblin and old Chief Thomas stepped in and stopped it. Hamblin explained that no one toward whom these Indians were not thoroughly friendly could witness a war dance with safety.

From Muddy to Vegas we had a drive of 63 miles across a desert, without a sprig of grass and with only some poisonous warm water at Kingston Springs about midway between. At Vegas lived the last band of Indians we would have to pass, and as they were understood to number but fifteen or twenty, and we had been so much annoyed and so often threatened by the red devils, my mess of five men determined that we would exterminate this band, if they annoyed us, and push on to California before those in our rear heard of it.

But we reckoned without our host. As we were preparing to start out on our afternoon and all night drive the keen eye of Chief Thomas caught on the fact that about 130 of the Indians were missing. He knew also that they had all been more or less dissatisfied with his decision to let us pass. He spoke to Hamblin about the matter and decided to send some of his swiftest young runners along in our wagons, to be let out two or three miles short of Kingston Springs and run ahead to scour the tops of a narrow box canyon we had to pass through and to command the absent Indians, if there, to desist. As a further precaution, he sent Chief Isaac along with us as far as the danger point. Leaving the Muddy about the middle of the afternoon we passed through the canyon in safety and stopped at Kingston Springs about midnight. Here Isaac and the young Indians turned back.

With a feeling of security that we had passed all danger, we drove rapidly over a smooth, hard, down-grade toward Vegas. Some years before the Mormons had established a settlement at Vegas and built a fort for its protection, a heavy stone wall, 25 feet high, 150 feet square, with wagon way through the south wall and a small gateway or door to the east. Inside, against the south wall, adobe dwellings had been constructed in the large courtyard. After the abandonment of this settlement the Indians had burned out all the woodwork about the fort. The ground round about indicated that the Spaniards had cultivated the soil some centuries prior and a large acreage still bore mission grape vines.

Before reaching this fort we had to drive half a mile across a level valley covered with grass and overgrown with mesquite or tornillo trees. I was driving the lead team, with four other young and well armed Americans in the wagon, all brave, determined and resolute young fellows, and as we entered the valley just before sun rise and saw the fort on higher ground beyond we began to congratulate one another that we would not have to submit to any more insolence from Indians when suddenly we came upon a group of fifty of them, seated on the grounding a circle about thirty steps from the road, each with a wolf skin filled with arrows strapped upon his back, and each with his face made hideous with war paint. Here was evidently a part of the "lost tribe" from the Muddy. A little further on we passed another group of about seventy, similarly seated, armed and painted. We were "in for it again."

I drove rapidly to the fort, entered it, unhitched the mules and turned them out to graze. Instantly every inside dwelling and every aperture thereto and in the outer wall were filled with armed Indians in war paint. They were hideous looking devils. Many had their faces equally divided, some longitudinally and some laterally, by a straight line, one half painted jet black and the other blood red. One big, burly fellow, who appeared to be a sort of boss, or sub-chief, and who took command of the wagon way through the south wall, had the whole of his ample face painted jet black, except a red and yellow spatter in the center of the fore-head, from which a red streak ran down to the center of the nose giving him the appearance of having been shot in the forehead with a small bullet, and from the wound the brains and blood had oozed out and the blood run down half the length his nose and coagulated in a large drop.

Directly the other teams arrived, and were driven inside, unharnessed and turned out without opposition, but no man was allowed to go outside, except Jake Humblin. Soon after breakfast Hamblin left the fort and we did not see him again until nearly sunset. The Indians stood there all day, and not a word was spoken. I tried to play "innocence" on the big, black fellow with the bullet wound in the forehead. Just outside of the south wall a beautiful stream of clear water trickled past. Procuring a cup, I walked to the wagon way through the wall and, smiling and hailing the big black fellow with "How! How!" (The usual Indian greeting), attempted to step outside to the stream. Seizing me by the shoulders with both hands he wheeled me about and with a loud grunt gave me a violent shove back into the fort.

We could not imagine what they were waiting for, nor did we find out till nearly night, but we got every shot ready for instant action when the attack should come, and my mess arranged a plan of attack as well as defense. My wagon stood facing one of the small-dismantled dwellings inside the wall. This was crowded with Indians. I had a double- barreled shotgun of unusually large caliber, besides a rifle and six-shooter. Into each barrel of this huge shotgun I put four inches of powder, twelve six-shooter balls and a handful of buckshot. I filled each tube with powder and put on carefully selected and fresh caps. Sitting in the wagon, the cover of which would to some extent protect me from arrows fired from the wagon way and from the east gate, I was to pour shots in through the inner door and windows of the dwelling, and instantly at the close of the bombardment my four companions were to charge the room with six-shooters, axes and hatchets, so that they could secure the protection of its walls. How I was to get across the open space between the wagon and the house after they should capture the latter was a question neither, asked or considered.

But I had been driving all night and was sleepy, while the others had slept on the road. It was then suggested by myself that I go to sleep in the wagon, with my gun in hand, take off one boot and put John Garber (the little Dutchman, who was scarcely considered in a fight) in front part of the wagon to watch the Indians closely and at sight of the first quick or suspicious movement among them to seize me by the big toe of my bootless foot and to give it a violent twist, so as to fully awaken me that I might go to shooting before the Indians could charge us. With this arrangement agreed to I went to sleep and I slept soundly until near sunset, when Jake Hamblin, Ira Hatch (a Mormon who lived with the Vegas tribe) and the Chief of the Vegas band arrived in the fort.

When Hamblin left the fort that morning he learned that the Indians were waiting for the signal to attack from the Chief of the Vegas band, and that the chief was at camp about three miles below the fort. Hamblin knew also that Ira Hatch, who had been sent on a mission to the Navajo tribe in Arizona, and who had great influence with the Chief and all the Vegas band, as well as with the 130 Muddy Indians who had joined them, was fully due at Vegas, and doubting his own influence with the chief and this out-lying band, he sought for Hatch that the latter might save us. The first buck he inquired of told him the Navajoes had killed Hatch; another said the Navajoes had eaten Hatch's animals so that he could not get back, while a third said Hatch had left early that morning by a cut-off trail for the Muddy, en route to Salt Lake City to report the result of his mission. It was certain the Indians were lying, and Hamblin inferred that Hatch was somewhere in the vicinity, and these Indians feared, if he found him, Hatch would stop the killing and they would miss the plunder. Five hundred yards below the fort Hamblin came upon a Vegas boy concealed in a bunch of grape vines. Drawing his six-shooter he coolly presented it at the boy's head and told him if he did not tell him where Hatch was he would kill him. The boy promptly replied that Hatch was down at the camp. Hamblin proceeded to the camp and interviewed the Chief, who told him Hatch had left that morning for the Muddy, and obdurately refused to listen to any proposition looking to our release.

Hamblin continued to argue and plead with the Chief, but in vain, until the middle of the afternoon, and then, not wishing to witness the massacre himself, took a stroll down through the Indian Village. In passing an open teepee he discovered Hatch lying asleep inside. He awakened him and apprised him of the situation. The chief had been waiting for Hatch to leave by the cut-off, and the Indians at the fork had been waiting for the chief. Hatch at once sought the chief and appealed to him to release us in accordance with the wishes of "Brother Brigham." "No!" He then consulted Hamblin as to our capacity to pay, who told the chief if he would release us we would give him in the way of ransom a fat mule (to eat), clothing, ammunition, tobacco, etc., aggregating in value about $500. "No;" he would kill us, take all we had, and no thanks to us. Hatch threatened him personally, but in vain.

At last, however, Hatch struck a soft spot and the old savage relented. Hatch said to him; "I know it is hard for you to let such rich plunder Escape, but if you will do so Brother Brigham will heap honors upon you. I am now on my way to Salt Lake City; Tutsegovet is old, and will tell Brother Brigham what a sacrifice you made to comply with his wishes and he will make you Big Chief south of the Rim of the Basin". That settled our fate, and late in the afternoon Hatch, Hamblin and the Chief came up to the fort. The chief greeted us cordially, shook hands with each of us, and made a speech, through the interpreter asking us to rest easy that night and not attempt to slip away, but to start next day openly and freely, as if nothing had happened.

I was still a little uneasy myself, but suggested to the chief that the women of the party were nervous and frightened, with all these armed and painted Indians hovering about them, whereupon he said he would withdraw them, except half a dozen to see that we did not attempt to sneak away in the night, and that on the morrow they would return to bid us good-by.

After peace was declared I counted the arrows in the wolf skin on the back of the big, black buck with the bullet wound in the forehead. There were 132 of them, some with iron and some with flint points while all were heavily poisoned. Some Indians use a combination of animal, vegetable and mineral poisons, for which there is no antidote, and the slightest wound from an arrow dipped in such a combination is almost certain death. The Piute Indians of Southern Utah, however, used only rattlesnake poison, for which there are many antidotes. Their mode of preparation and application of the poison was about as follows; Take the liver or lungs (or both) of an animal; find a rattlesnake and stir him up with a pole until he is "fighting mad", and then poke the liver at him until he bites it as often as he can eject poison from his fangs. The poisoned liver and lungs are then placed in an earthern vessel with a little water, and kept up to about blood heat until the whole becomes a mass of poisonous jelly. Into this the arrow is dipped until the point and the fine thews that bind it to the arrow are thoroughly coated with the poison, and then it is laid aside to dry. When an arrow thus prepared penetrates the flesh or even breaks the skin, more or less of the poison is communicated to the blood, and either death or disability soon follows.

While the five wagons and us were being held in this precarious position in this old fort for ten hours by at least 150 Indian warriors, all heavily armed with poisoned arrows, I was able to make a pretty good mental analysis of the peculiar and exceptional fear that Indian warfare inspires in the white man. I found that it was not because the Indians are better or braver or more resolute and determined and persistent fighters than whites; they are far from it; for there is infinitely more danger in fighting whites than Indians; but I found, not only from this, but from other similar adventures, that the peculiar and exceptional fear of Indians is inspired by the knowledge of the absolute certainty of death in case you are captured, maimed or defeated. The fear of torture is also an element usually uppermost in the mind, although comparatively few of the western tribes ever resorted to torture. The Chiricahua Apaches were the most fiendish Indians ever on this continent in this respect, and the more heroic the fight a man put up against them the longer and more cruelly would he be tortured; while some of the old Atlantic tribes had the highest admiration for a man who put up a heroic fight, however many of them he might kill, and if he was wounded in such a fight they would nurse him back to life and release him.

Early next morning the whole 150 bucks and a few handsome young squaws of light color and tattooed chins, appeared in the fort with clean and smiling faces, and each one of the whole mongrel breed had to extend the glad hand to each one of our party, including the two ladies. We hitched up, bid them goodbye, and drove away, reaching San Bernardino, Cal., the sixth day afterwards meeting many Mormon families along the Mojave and about Cajon Pass who had sacrificed their rich farms and fine orchards and vineyards in San Bernardino valley in order to comply with the order of Brigham Young that all the faithful must go to Zion.

In San Bernardino we found most of the strong Texas party who had made forced marches down through Utah to overtake the Perkins party. They were puzzled to know how they had missed the Perkins people, and were anxious to know what had become of them. When we told them the story of the massacre they were profoundly shocked and became bitterly hostile toward the Mormons who had not yet gotten away from San Bernardino. When we came to compare dates and events with these Texans, it became plain that the massacre occurred on the very day that Jake Hamblin took them off the road at that point and let their wagons down the mountain by ropes.

A day or two after our arrival Old Daddy Hunt, who was a sort of privileged character, was standing in the middle of the street in front of a cottage saloon with a front and back door open and the counter between. Hunt was a pursy and pompous old fellow, and while discussing the futility of the government trying to fight the Mormons he slapped himself upon his ample stomach and said; "Why I wouldn't be a bit afraid to stand up facing a whole regiment of those troops at Fort Bridger and let them fire at me point blank, for I know the Lord would turn the bullets aside". At that a tall, determined looking fellow of the already deeply angered Texas party pushed his coat back from his shooter and remarked; "I believe I will just try the Lord with one shot myself, you old bag of wind." But before he could draw his gun Daddy Hunt, who had suddenly lost faith in the Lord, was sailing high in the air above the cottage saloon counter and going through the back door like a shot out of a gun. Nor was he ever seen in San Bernardino afterward, as he probably left that night for Zion.

The Execution, of John D. Lee

On March 13th, 1877 before his execution, Lee had written: "I feel composed and as calm as a summer morning. I hope to meet my fate with manly courage. I declare my innocence. I have done nothing designedly wrong in that unfortunate and lamentable affair with which I have been implicated. I used my utmost endeavors to save them from their sad fate. I would freely have given worlds, were they at my command, to have averted that evil. Death to me has no terror. It is but a struggle and all is over. I know I have a reward in heaven, and my conscience does not accuse me."

On March 23rd, Lee was brought to Mountain Meadows, the scene of the massacre twenty years before, to be shot for his crime. In the twenty years since the massacre the green valley of Mountain Meadows had changed to an arid plain. The luxuriant vegetation that had clothed it twenty years before was gone. The springs were dry. Only here and there a copse of sagebrush or scrub oak served to make the desolation still more desolate.

With Lee was a party of armed men, who alighted from their wagons and approached the site of the massacre. Among them were the United States Marshal, the District Attorney, a military guard, and some private citizens. Over the wheels of one of the wagons, blankets served as a screen for the firing party. Lee took his seat on the rough pine board coffin.

Then the Marshall read the order: "Mr. Lee, if you have anything to say before the order of the court is carried into effect, you can do so now."

Rising from the coffin, Lee with unfaltering voice said: "I have little to say this morning. It seems I have to be made a victim; a victim must be had, and I am the victim. I studied to make Brigham Young's will my pleasure for thirty years. See now what I have come to this day. I have been sacrificed in a cowardly, dastardly manner. I cannot help it; it is my last word and it is so. I ask the Lord my God, if my labors are done, to receive my spirit."

A Methodist clergyman (Parson Stokes) then knelt by Lee's side and offered a brief prayer. After shaking hands with those around him, Lee removed a part of his clothing. He handed his hat to the Marshal, who bound a handkerchief over Lee's eyes, his hands being free at his own request. Then seating himself with his face to the firing party, hands clasped over his head, he exclaimed, "Let them shoot the balls through my heart. Don't let them mangle my body."

The command from Nelson was given, "READY, AIM, FIRE!"

Five soldiers fired, and John D. Lee fell back on his coffin without a cry. Only the echoes answered throughout the surrounding hills, and then their was ever lasting silence in the meadow.

The foregoing (chapters) constitute the chief incidents of interest that came under my personal observation during my eventful trip across the continent in the tragic year of 1857-58, as I recall them to memory after forty-six years of a busy life on the Pacific Frontier, and I present them in the hope that their perusal may interest all who read the foregoing.

Captain John I. Ginn

The Journal

EVANSVILLE, INDIANA. FRIDAY, JULY 13, 1877.

THE MOUNTAIN MEADOWS MASSACRE.

Brigham Young's Personal connection with
The Massacre of The Gentiles.

Springfield, Ills., July 12—Captain John Tobin, formerly President of California, later of St. Louis, and still later of Springfield, will be one of District Attorney Howard's principal witnesses to prove Brigham Young's personal connection with the massacre of the Gentiles.

His name is mentioned in Lee's confession. He tells a long story, which is in substance that having gained the confidence of Brigham by aiding Mormon emigrants, he was appointed Instructor of the Territorial Militia, which position he resigned because squads of the cavalry were used as avengers.

Subsequently he undertook to guide a party of three strong, outspoken anti-Mormons to California, but the party was overtaken by a band of mounted Mormons, led by Brigham Young, Jr., and compelled to stop, under pretence that they were going to California to misrepresent Mormonism.

They finally proceeded, but were continually dogged by the Mormons, who at length fought them as they were encamping at night and massacreing them. The party were left for dead, and the Mormons, taking their horses, rode away.

Sixty hours afterwards, the United States mail wagon and a party en route to San Bernardino, took them up, but two died soon after. Tobin had a shot in the right eye, which nearly mad him blind. He claims to have important documentary evidence of plotting against the government and the Gentiles of the party of Brigham Young.

Author's collection.

AUTHORS NOTES

The balance of Ginn's Journal or manuscript consists of a recitation of various Indian battles, which he presumes to have been incited by the activities of Mormon missionaries among the Indians. He also gives a history of the origin of Mormonism. The balance of his manuscript, consisting altogether of 106 pages, has been taken from various official sources, and shows a great deal of careful research. However, it contains only a few references to his personal experiences, and these only will be copied where they throw light on the foregoing narrative.

Chapter VI—Mormonism, The Origin and Atrocities. Speaks of the number of Mormons in 1900s, the manuscript is presumed to have been written in 1903.

Chapter VII—The Mormon Rebellion. (Read bottom Footnote.)
"Many of these trains (of supplies) reached Utah, on the Big sandy, Green River and Ham's Fork, ahead of the Tenth Infantry, the advance regiment of the army, but the Mormons did not molest them until after the army came up."

[##]on Lot Smith: describes Lot's death identically the same as the story was told to (ALTER) by Philip Johnston, whose father was there

---

[##] November 27th, 1857, George Gibbs, Esq., of Washington Territory, wrote to General N.S. Clarks, Commander of the Department of the Pacific, as follows;

"A very curious statement was recently made to me by some of the Indians near Steilacoom. They said that the Klikatats had told them that Choosuklee (Jesus Christ) had recently appeared on the other side of the mountains; that he was after awhile coming here, when the whites would be sent out of the country, and all would be well for themselves. It needed only a little reflection to connect this Second Advent with the visit of Brigham Young to the Flathead and Nez Perces Country." December 1st, 1857, Captain Kirkham wrote from Walla Walla, Washington; "The Snakes, who are in direct communication with the Mormons, tell our Indians that they are at the time. Where did Ginn learn of it? Captain Smith, a wagon master with Reno's command, and had been Captain of the Missouri Militia that killed Joe Smith. While out hunting, sage hens with a soldier named McNeil, he was captured by Lot Smith. He talked so agreeable, that Lot let him go, but kept McNeil. The latter then told Lot who Captain Smith was. McNeil was thrown in jail in Salt Lake, where he remained until the army marched through. He then started suit against Brigham Young for having him confined. During the trial McNeil was kept under heavy guard. One day, returning from trial, he was shot from ambush, on the street, falling dead between his guards.

---

well supplied with ammunition and that they can get from the Mormons any quantity that they wish; and they further tell our Indians that the Mormons are anxious to supply them, to-wit; The Nez Perces, The Cayuses and Walla-Wallas, with everything that they wish. I would not be surprised if the Mormon influence should extend to all the tribes in our neighborhood, and if they are determined to fight we may have trouble among the Indians on the coast again." January 1st, 1858. General Clarke reported to the Headquarters of the Army that the Indians about San Bernardino, Southern California, had joined the Mormons in their recent exodus to Utah; that from Carson Valley (then in Carson county, Utah, but now in western Nevada) where there were Mormon settlements, "we have like reports of the ill effects on the Indians of Mormon influence, and that from various sections of Southern California where the Mormons could and doubtless had tampered with the Indians, the latter had become so insolent that the white inhabitants had become alarmed."

January 30th, 1858, Major R. S. Garnett of the Ninth Infantry Commanding Fort Simcoe, Washington Territory, reported to the Department of the Pacific as follows: "It seems proper that I should report, for the information of General Clarke, that the Indian Chief Skloom, brother of Kamia Kin, has recently sent word to me, for the second time, that the Mormons on one or two occasions since last summer have sent emissaries among the Indians of this region to incite them to a union with the Mormons in hostility to the United States.

He states that the Chiefs repel these overtures from the Mormons but that some of the young men seem disposed to countenance them.

The Mormons make them large promises of arms, ammunition, cattle etc". U.S. Message and Documents." 1857.

The Mountain Meadows Massacre was executed four days before martial law had been declared in Salt Lake.

Hamblin says that he had 100 head of Perkins party or (Fancher party) cattle on his ranch when he (Ginn) passed through, but gave them up the following year to relatives of the murdered people. (Cites no proof.)

The Parovan Indians never heard of the spring being poisoned at Corn Creek until it reached them from Salt Lake City. "But one man is known to have escaped from the beleaguered emigrants camp, and he was pursued by Ira Hatch, Prime Coleman and two other Mormons named Young, all of whom Doubtless participated in the massacre, more than 100 miles, beyond the Muddy, where he was wandering about, wounded, nearly starved and in a demented condition. His throat was promptly cut and he was buried in the sand."

This "one man" (William Baker) corresponds with the reports first brought to Los Angeles.

"If an American was clad in well-worn clothing, with long and un-kept hair, and was particularly dirty (as was often the case after a long trip across the plains), he could very readily pass himself of upon the Indians as a Mormon only so long as he could avoid shaking hands with any of them. The first party of Americans or Gentiles known to have passed over the ground after the massacre at Mountain Meadows consisted of seven men, beside four or five Mormons who furnished them with transportation from Salt Lake City to San Bernardino, California. Although five of the seven were young at that time, some of these men were keen and trained observers, and made diligent, inquiries, both from whites and Indian Mormons, all the way from Salt Lake City until they passed out of the Indian country, 450 miles to the southward. They passed over the scene of the massacre about three weeks after the butchery, and while the bodies of the men, women and children butchered were still in a state of almost perfect preservation. From all they could learn, by inquiry and observation, they were forced to the conclusion that the Mormons alone and the very heads of the church themselves were responsible for that most atrocious and cowardly crime."

In the above paragraph Ginn refers to himself and party, which consisted of 11 or 12 men (five Gentiles) and two women. He claims to have been the first to pass through, although he certainly must have read the stories already current in the California papers when he arrived.

Ginn claims that the first group of emigrants were shot down, and then the Mormons lost their courage, ceased to fire. After a consultation it was decided they must all die, to prevent exposure, then the second group, which had marched a mile further, was killed. This seems logical, particularly in view of the fact that Ginn saw women and children in the group nearest the spring, showing that the men and women were not entirely segregated.

"It will be seen from his testimony before Major Carleton (which was a palpable whitewash of the Mormons) that Jack Hamblin said he got to his home at the north end of the Mountain Meadows on the 16th of Sept., exactly one week after the emigrants were killed. But instead of reaching home on that date from the north, as he says, he doubtless reached there from the south where he had gone to conduct a strong Texas train (which he took off the road and around the scene of the massacre on the very day it occurred) as far south as the Muddy, about 100 miles. It would have taken him just about one week to go to the Muddy with the Texas train and return by saddle or buggy. That he took this Texas train off from a good road and out through the woods and over mountains where they had to let their wagons down by taking a hitch around a tree by strong ropes, to keep this strong and well armed party of Texans from any knowledge of the desperate condition of the Perkins party or (Fancher party), is conclusive proof that Jake Hamblin had foreknowledge of what was to occur on that Mountain Meadows that day.

This, then, explains why the Mormons were so quick to set the date of the massacre on Sept.7th, one week ahead, instead of Sept. 18th, the day on which it was to occur. Jake says he got home Sept. 16th, which would be two days before the massacre, the final massacre, took place…

Ben F. Ficklin, a mountaineer, was sent by Gen. Johnson to the Flathead country to procure horses and cattle for the army. He failed to get any, as both mountaineers and Indians were afraid to attempt to drive the stock, for fear of being robbed by the Mormons. While he was absent, the Bannocks attacked a Mormon settlement at the mouth of the Blackfoot creek, on the Snake River. Claimed Mormons had furnished arms to the Nez Perce, with which the latter had attacked the Bannocks.

Chapter VIII—Indian wars incited by Mormons...

"Many Mormons doubted Ira Hatch's fealty to the church, and suspected he was pretending to be loyal to the faith until such time as he would be afforded an opportunity to "get even" for the assassination of his brother, whom Bill Hickman, one of the four captains of Danites or Destroying Angels, had shot in the back of the head while young Hatch was lying face down drinking from a spring of water. But Brother Ira seems to have been faithful to the last."

Follows with story of the Spokane, pelouse and Coeur d' Alene war under Col. Steptoe.

Chapter IX—The Navajo War...(1858)...the results of Ira Hatch's mission.

Chapter X—From Rev. Larry Preston, on what his Great-great Grandfather over heard in Brigham Young's office?

CHAPTER VI

Mormonism-The Origin and Atrocities.

During the first seven years of the great overland migration to California, punctuated as it was by Indian massacres and death from privation and accidents, it will probably be well within the bounds of truth to say that during the whole of those seven years there were not so many violent deaths nor so much intense suffering from hunger and cold among men and animals as in the single year of 1857. The reason for this was, except at the two small military posts of Fort Kearney in Nebraska and Fort Laramie in Wyoming, there was not a friendly face on the road between Fort Leavenworth on the Missouri river and the Summit of the Sierra Nevada Range in California. Theretofore emigrants and military expeditions could confidently count on replenishing their work animals and other supplies in Utah, nearly midway of their journey, but in 1857 the Mormons were in rebellion against the Government and exceedingly hostile toward all Gentile emigrants.

Prior to 1857, whatever might be the disposition of the wild tribes of Indians east of Utah, as the Sioux, Cheyennes, Arapahoes and Blackfeet, once emigrants reached the Mormon settlements in the valleys of Utah they were safe, except along the northern route through Nevada, where in early years they were subject to attack from the Pah Utahs (or Piutes, as the name has become corrupted) along the Humboldt River.

The Utahs of northern and eastern Utah, the Parovans in the central portion of the territory, and the Pah Utahs (or Water Utahs) further south had early become converted to Mormonism, and were as completely under the control of the church authorities of that sect as were the white Mormons. This held good in 1857 also, and hence if emigrants escaped the vengeance of the saints they would be harassed and held up by the Indians until the armed and organized militia of the saints could come up and kill them. By this process was the Mountain Meadow Massacre perpetrated.

A brief history of Mormonism is necessary to a full understanding of what follows of why they were "persecuted" in the eastern states, as they claimed, why they went to Utah, and why they went into rebellion, and why they so treacherously and mercilessly butchered 136 unarmed men, women and children at Mountain Meadows, September, 11th, 1857.

Mormonism originated with Joseph Smith, who was born in Sharon, Vermont, December 23rd, 1805. At the age of ten years he removed with his parents to Palmyra, N. Y. where he falsely claimed that on the night of September 21st, 1823, the angel Moroni revealed to him the existence and whereabouts of the Book of Mormon engraved in some unknown hieroglyphics on plates of gold and deeply buried in undisturbed ground in the side of the hill Cumorah. This he claimed to have translated, and published the nonsense in 1830.

Smith's alleged translation from the gold plates was undoubtedly a fraud, as his method was most favorable to fraud. He had four witnesses (including the young woman he afterwards married) present to write down the words as he pretended to read them off from the gold plates or sheets, Martin Harris, a farmer; Oliver Coudry, a country school teacher; David Whitmer, a merchant and Emma Hale, who afterwards became the Prophet's wife, all of whom testified to "all nations, kindred's, tongues and peoples", until the day of their respective deaths, that they had seen the golden plates upon which were engraved the hieroglyphics, but not one of whom ever claimed that he or she knew the meaning of a single character so engraved. The original manuscript of the Book of Mormon, as thus written out by the people named and as dictated by Joseph Smith, is now the property of George W. Schweich of Richmond, Missouri, a grandson of David Whitmer, one of the amanuenses who wrote it. The Polygamous Mormons or Brighamites have made repeated efforts to get hold of this manuscript, and have offered as high as $100,000 cash for it. It covers 600 large sheets of linen paper the size of fools-cap, closely written on both sides, and contains 350,000 words. Now as to the fraudulent translation; Smith did not read from the plates direct. He put his Urim and Thummim (a piece of obsidian, or volcanic glass, a seer's stone, into a deep hat into which he (but not the others) looked. He claimed that the inside of the hat was made supernaturally light and there appeared to him a scroll with the Greek like characters engraved thereon and beneath them a translation in English which he read off to the scribes. But all this time Smith was doubtless reading from the religious romance written by Solomon Spaulding about 1810, the manuscript of which had fallen into Smith's hands and which manuscript he doubtless had open before him, but concealed from the others by the hat. The translation was not finished until 1829, soon after which it was published in book form, Martin Harris, the dupe farmer, furnishing the money to pay for the printing.

The Book of Mormon was really a sort of religious romance, written about 1810 by the one Solomon Spaulding, to account for the presence of Indians on this Continent when it was first visited by Europeans.

The real author of the Book of Mormon was therefore Solomon Spaulding, a graduate of Dartmouth College, who became a clergyman and resided at Cherry Vale, in the State of New York, until his health failed. He was distinguished for a lively imagination and a great fondness for history. From Cherry Vale N. Y. Mr. Spaulding and his wife removed to New Salem, Ashtabula County, Ohio, and there his health so far failed him that he retired from active labor as a minister. In and about the town of New Salem there were numerous mounds or forts, supposed by many to be the dilapidated dwellings and fortification of an extinct race. The north American Indians suggested the idea to Mr. Spaulding that they were the descendants of the lost ten tribes of Israel, and this afforded a good ground work for his history, tale or novel. For three years he labored on this work, which he entitled "The Manuscript Found".

Mormon and his son Moroni, who act so large a part in Joseph Smith's Book of Mormon, were two of the principal characters in it. The extreme artiquity of Mr. Spaulding's subject led him to write in the most ancient style and, as the Old Testament is among the most ancient books of the world, he imitated its style as nearly as possible. His sole object in writing this imaginary history was to amuse himself and his neighbors, to whom he delighted to read it, as his widow (who afterwards married a Mr. Davison) and other members of his family frequently testified.

In 1812 (when Joseph Smith was but seven years of age) Spalding's manuscript of the original Book of Mormon was presented to a printer or book publisher named Patterson, living in Pittsburgh, Pa., with a view to its publication. Before any satisfactory arrangements could be made the author died, and the manuscript remained in the possession of Mr. Patterson apparently unnoticed and uncared for. Patterson died in 1825, having previously loaned the manuscript to one Sideny Rigdon, a printer or type-setter in his employ. This Sidney Rigdon appropriated the work of the deceased Solomon Spaulding to his own use and, joining fortunes with Joseph Smith and organizing the new sect, at once became, next to Joseph Smith, the principal leader of the Mormons.

Thus upon this romance, woven from the lively imagination of a retired scholar, and stolen by one of the founders, was instituted a new creed which has allured to its position of power and pelf a few intellectual men and drawn into its skillfully prepared meshes hundreds of thousands of the ignorant and superstitious of Europe and America.

The first principal of this creed, from its foundation by Smith to the present day, appears to have been embraced in two resolutions;

"Resolved, 1st. That the earth and the fullness thereof belong to the Lord and His Saints".

"2nd. that we are His Saints".

Or, in a nut-shell; "Everything there is belongs to us".

April 6th, 1830, the Mormon Church was formally established, at Manchester, Ontario County, N.Y. and in June of that year had a membership of thirty men and women.

In January 1831, Smith and his followers removed to Kirtland, Ohio, where they numbered upward of 1,000. Here they began to put in practice the first principle of their creed, and March 23rd , 1832, Smith and his colleague, Sidney Rigdon, were dragged from their beds by the people whom they had swindled by fraudulent banking and other operations, and were tarred and feathered.

The Mormons were joined at Kirtland by Brigham Young in 1832, Brigham having been born at Whitingham, Vermont, June 1st, 1801.

In 1838 Smith and Rigdon fled from Ohio and took refuge in Missouri, settling near Independence, Jackson County, where there was already a Mormon gathering. Owing to the practice of the "first principle" of the creed by the Saints, the sturdy pioneers of the backwoods soon rose in arms and the Mormons were driven out.

From there they went north to the Far West, Caldwell County, where another Mormon Community had settled. At the close of the year, owing to the hostile attitude of the Mormons, who had armed themselves and gathered in open resistance to the people who refused to be robbed in the name of the Lord, the militia of Missouri was called out. Smith and Rigdon were arrested on charges of treason, murder and felony. The Mormons capitulated and agreed to emigrate to Illinois. Rigdon was released on a writ of habeas corpus, and Smith broke jail and followed the congregation across the Mississippi to Nauvoo, Illinois, where the foundation of the Mormon temple was laid in 1841. The Book of Mormon inferentially condemns polygamy, but in 1843, at Nauvoo, Joseph Smith, the prophet and revelator, announced that pernicious doctrine authorized by revelation. That was based on God's promise to Abraham to make his seed more numerous than the sands of the sea shore and Smith wanted to raise up enough soldiers to defy all opposition.

On the 6th of May, 1844, the Expositor, a newspaper in opposition to polygamy and the practice of Smith and his followers, was mobbed by the Mormons and destroyed, and the 27th of the following month Joseph Smith and his brother Hiram were killed by a mob who broke into jail at Carthage, where they were confined for the mobbing of the Expositor office.

Their trouble continuing, on account of their evil practices, in the autumn of 1846 Brigham Young, who had succeeded Joseph Smith as head of the church and chief prophet, led the Mormons out of Illinois and across the country to Council Bluffs, Iowa, where they remained until the spring of 1847, when the new leader took them out over the western plains to settle in the fertile valleys of Utah, hoping thereby to get out of the jurisdiction of the United States.

But as fate would have it, that same year (1847) Mexico ceded Utah to the United States; so that there was no hope left for Brigham for the establishment of his cherished idea of an hierocracy than to build up such power, by the active practice of polygamy and the flooding of the illiterate and ignorant slums of Europe by proselyting missionaries, as would enable him, in time, to defy and defeat any army the United States might be able to send out so far from its base of supplies and re-enforcements.

This he made his deluded followers believe he had done in 1857, but the sequel shows very plainly that Brigham Young himself did not believe it, for he had his friends and agents in Washington induce President Buchanan to appoint a commission to proceed to Salt Lake City early in the spring of 1858 that he (Brigham) might negotiate a peace with them while Johnston's army was still snowbound behind the rugged Wasatch mountains.

It is probable, also, that when Brigham Young first made his bluff he was presuming on the depleted condition of the regular army, as on the 1st of July, 1857, the army consisted of but 15,764 men, and these had to garrison 68 forts of a large and permanent character, and to occupy 70 posts less permanently established but where the presence of a force was absolutely required, and these forts and posts were spread over an area embracing a circuit of 3,000,000 square miles. The Kansas troubles also necessited the presence of a large number of troops in that territory and, as will be seen from official sources later on, Mormon agents were fomenting hostilities among the Indians of California, Oregon and Washington territories at the same time.

The name adopted by the Mormons was the "Church of Jesus Christ of Latter Day Saints". Soon after the Mormon rebellion of 1857 and prior to the passage by Congress of laws prohibiting the beastly practice of polygamy, a strong opposition to polygamy had grown up in the church itself, and this resulted in the organization of a protestant Mormon church, called the "Re-organized Church of Jesus Christ of Latter Day Saints". This sect has grown to be quite numerous, practices honesty, lives in peace and harmony with their neighbors in the United States, Canada, Europe and Australia, and holds the "Adam God" worship, blood atonement and polygamy, as taught by the "Brighamites," to be heretical. This innocuous sect now has temples or fine church edifices and flourishing congregations in the principle eastern towns from which the evil-doers of the old church were driven out nearly three-quarters of a century ago. As at Independence, Missouri, and the famous old temple at Kirtland, Ohio, from which Joseph Smith, Sidney Rigdon and Brigham Young were driven out in 1838. The headquarters of the reorganized and really Christian sect of Mormons are at Lamoni, Iowa, where one of its principle churches is located. However much these (then unorganized) people might have been opposed to the rebellion of 1857, it would have cost them their lives to have-made it known at that time.

It would seem that there is nothing too absurd in constitution or ridiculous in origin for men and women to believe and become infatuated with if it is only labeled "religion".

Under this label the rankest poison will be gulped down with as great facility and avidity as if it were an oyster. The number of Mormons in the United States was but 166,125 in 1890, while in 1900 this had increased to 300,000 to 345,000 of the blood atonement, polygamous "Brighamites," and 45,000 of the Re-organized Church of Jesus Christ of Latter Day Saints, all of the latter as sincerely believing in the divinity and inspiration of Joseph Smith's fraudulent claims as the others. There are also five large Mormon Colonies in Mexico, four in the State of Chihuahua and one in Sonora, besides many individual Mormons scattered throughout the republic, probably aggregating 25,000, all of the Brighamites branch. They have never attempted to openly violate the laws of Mexico by plural marriages; but after taking one wife under the civil law (the only legal marriage in Mexico) they may add as many "housekeepers" to their harems as they please, their female dupes being satisfied with a (secret) church marriage, which is no marriage at all under the laws of that republic. It is safe to predict that when they shall have built up "The Kingdom" to sufficient strength in that country they will give the Government a world of trouble, for to their doctrines and teachings there is nothing more abhorrent than the civil restraints which civilization imposes upon mankind.

By states the United States census for 1890 gave the following Mormons; Alabama, 572; Arizona, 6,500; Arkansas, 60; California, 1,393; Colorado, 1,762; Connecticut, 8; Florida, 257; Georgia, 175; Idaho, 14,972; Illinois, 1,909; Indiana, 380; Indian Territory, 46; Iowa, 5,303; Kansas, 1,106; Kentucky, 249; Maine, 442; Maryland, 75; Massachusetts, 457; Michigan, 1,540; Minnesota, 224;

Mississippi, 197; Missouri, 3,189; Montana, 122; Nebraska, 1,058; Nevada, 525; New Jersey, 21; New Mexico 456; New York, 158; North Carolina, 108; Ohio, 10,678; Oregon, 95; Pennsylvania, 417; Rhode Island, 233; South Carolina, 203; South Dakota, 88; Tennessee, 198; Texas, 437; Utah, 118,201; Virginia 171; Washington, 34; West Virginia, 406; Wisconsin, 341; Wyoming, 1,386.

In 1890 there were no Mormons in Alaska, Delaware, the District of Columbia, Louisiana, New Hampshire, North Dakota, Oklahoma or Vermont. Yet four of the greatest leaders and practically the founders of the church were born in Vermont, Joseph Smith, Brigham Young, John Taylor and General Daniel H. Wells. The three first named, and in the order named, were the first three Presidents of the church. In 1892 Mrs. General John A. Logan pronounced Mormonism a "menace to society and state." Gardinal Gibbons denounced it as "a plague spot on our civilization, a discredit to our Government, a degradation of the female sex and standing menace to the sanctity of the marriage bond," and Dr. Charles H. Parkhurst pronounced it a "peril."

CHAPTER VII

The Mormon Rebellion

In his annual report, dated December 5th, 1857, Secretary of War John B. Floyd devoted considerable space to the Mormon question, reciting the fact "that Utah was peopled almost exclusively by people of that sect; that they had then been for twelve months sending defiance to the sovereign power, and that, occupying as they did the great pathway leading from the Atlantic states to the new and flourishing communities growing up on the Pacific seaboard, they could no longer be allowed to menace emigration not only by extortion and massacre themselves but by encouraging, if not exciting, the nomad savages to acts of violence indiscriminately upon all ages, sexes and conditions of wayfarers, as well to hostility to the general government".

Therefore a body of troops had been sent to Utah, with the civil officers then recently appointed to that territory, the intention being merely to establish the civil functionaries in the offices to which they had been commissioned and to erect Utah into a geographical military department, where the troops could be called upon to act as a posse comitatus for the enforcement of federal laws and where they would be in a position favorable for holding the Indians in check throughout the whole circumjacent region of country. It was not as that time deemed within the line of reasonable probability that the Mormons would put themselves beyond the pale of reconciliation with the government by acts of unprovoked, open and wanton rebellion. But they did, in the face of positive assurances given them that the intention of the government in sending troops into the military department of Utah was entirely pacific.

Great care was taken in preparing for the march to Utah that nothing should be seen to excite apprehension of any action on the part of the army in the least conflicting with the fixed principles of our institutions, by which the military is strictly subordinate to the civil authority. The instructions to the commanding officer were deliberately considered and carefully drawn; and he was charged not to allow any conflict to take place between the troops and the people of the territory, except only in case he should be called upon by the governor for soldiers to act as a posse comitatus in enforcing obedience to the laws.

In conformity with this sentiment, and to assure the Mormon people of the real intention of the movement, Captain Stewart Van Vliet, a discreet and intelligent officer, was sent in advance of the army to Utah, arriving in Great Salt Lake City, on the 2nd of September, 1857, having left his teams and military escort at Ham's Fork, 143 miles east of the city. This he did by order of the Mormon military authorities; this not withstanding Captain Van Vleit had been instructed by General Scott, through Captain Alfred Pleasanton, to "impress upon the officer in charge of your escort the imperious necessity for a very careful circumspection of conduct in his command," and that "the men should not only be carefully selected for this service, but they should be repeatedly admonished never to comment upon or ridicule anything they may see or hear, and to treat the inhabitants of Utah with kindness and consideration". At that time neither the General-in-Chief nor Captain Pleasanton knew the savage and blood-thirsty nature of the religious fanatics whom they desired treated with such "kindness and consideration."

On his arrival at Great Salt Lake City Captain Van Vliet called upon Brigham Young and other influential Mormon leaders, delivering to the former a letter from General Scott setting forth the pacific object of the small army then en route. He also endeavored to allay their apprehension by assuring them that it was not the purpose or desire of the government or the army to molest any one for their religious opinions, however abhorrent those opinions might be to the principles of Christian morality. As for himself he was there for the purpose of purchasing supplies and having winter quarters prepared for the army.

Brigham Young replied, with the hearty approval of all the other leaders, that while they had plenty of supplies none would be sold to or for the army; that the Mormons had been persecuted, murdered and robbed in Missouri and Illinois, both by mob and state authorities, and that now the United States were about to pursue the same course, and that therefore he and the people of Utah had determined to resist all persecution at the commencement, and that the troops then on the march for Utah should not enter the Salt Lake Valley.

The seeming determination of the leaders to resist to the death the entrance of the troops into the valley caused Captain Van Vliet to tell them plainly and frankly what he conceived would be the result of such a course. He told them that they might prevent the small military force then approaching Utah from getting through the narrow defiles and rugged passes of the mountains that year, but that the next season the government would send troops sufficient to overcome all opposition.

The answer to this was invariably the same; "We are aware that such will be the case, but when those troops arrive they will find Utah to be a desert. Every house will be burned to the ground, every tree cut down, and every field laid waste. We have three years provisions on hand which we will "cache" and take to the mountains and bid defiance to all the powers of the government." (Van Vliet's official report.)

During his sojourn in the city Captain Van Vliet attended public services in the Tabernacle on Sunday, more than 4,000 Mormons being present. Elder John Taylor (who succeeded to the presidency of the church after the death of Brigham Young) preached a sermon in the course of which he referred to the approach of the troops and declared they should not enter the territory. He then referred to the probability of an over-powering force being sent against them and desired all present who would apply the torch to their own buildings, and cut down all their trees and lay waste their fields, to hold up their hands, when instantly up went every hand in an audience numbering over 4,000 persons. In the same discourse Apostle Taylor, said that none of the rulers of the earth were entitled to their positions unless appointed by the Lord, and that the Almighty had appointed a man to rule over and govern His Saints, and that man was Brigham Young and that they would have no one else to rule over them.

The day after Captain Van Vleit left on his return, Brigham Young, as Governor and Superintendent of Indian affairs for the territory of Utah, issued a proclamation, which was tantamount to a declaration of war against the United States. It was addressed "To the

Citizens of Utah," and in the preamble he claimed, "We are invaded by a hostile force who are evidently assailing us to accomplish our overthrow and destruction." He then recited that for the past twenty-five years they had "trusted officials of the government, from constables and justices to Judges, Governors and Presidents, only to be scorned, held in derision, insulted and betrayed;" alluded to their troubles in Missouri and Illinois; claimed that "our opponents have availed themselves of prejudice against us, because of our religious faith, to send out a formidable host to accomplish our destruction," and grew eloquent in this declaration; "We are condemned unheard, and forced to an issue with an armed mercenary mob which has been sent against us at the instigation of anonymous letter writers, ashamed to father the base, slanderous falsehoods which they have given to the public, or corrupt officials which have brought false accusations against us to screen themselves in their own infamy, and of hireling priests and howling editors who prostitute the truth for filthy lucre's sake." (Brigham's sermon published officially in Desert News.)

He therefore "forbid all armed forces of every description from coming into the territory under any pretense whatever;" ordered that "all the forces in said territory hold themselves in readiness to march at a moment's notice to repel any and all such invasion," and declared martial law to exist from and after September 15th, 1857, and no person shall be allowed to pass or re-pass into, or through, or from this territory without a permit from the proper officers."

Early in the summer of 1857 the Tenth Infantry under Colonel E. B. Alexander, the Fifth Infantry under Brevet Colonel C. A. Waite, and two batteries of artillery (twelve and six pounders) under Captain Reno of the Ordnance Department and Captain Phelps of the Fourth Artillery, had been started out from Fort Leavenworth on the long march across the plains to Utah.

General Wm. S. Harney, then commanding the department of Kansas, was designated commander of the expedition to Utah, and was to follow later with the Second Dragoons, of which regiment he was Colonel. Later in the season the political troubles of 1856 again broke out in Kansas, and the government deemed it advisable to retain General Harney in command of that territory. This necessitated still further delay, to designate an able and discreet officer to take command of the Utah expedition and to enable him to reach Fort Leavenworth and fit out for the long trip. Consequently it was not until the 28th of August that orders were issued from Washington for Colonel Albert Sidney Johnston of the Second Cavalry (then running the southern boundary line of Kansas) to repair to Leavenworth, fit out six companies of the Second Dragoons, take the civil officers for Utah with him and take command of the army sent out to put down the Mormon rebellion.

The instructions, prepared by the General-in-Chief (Winfield Scott) in concert with the War Department, for the guidance of the commander and the officers and men under him, were very specific, and enjoined them to obey all requisitions and summons from the civil governor, federal judges or marshals "where your military judgement and prudence do not forbid, nor compel you to modify in execution, the movement they may suggest," and above all, "in no case will you, your officers or men, attack any body of citizens whatever," except such requisition or summons, or in sheer self-defense."

It is evident that it was not the troops themselves that Brigham Young so much objected to and feared (as he stated to Captain Van Vliet) as it was to the new civil governor, judges and marshals, backed by the troops and the consequent loss to Brigham of the power and the perquisites he then enjoyed as an autocrat. He dreaded the civil law, and shuddered at the contemplation of its enforcement within his domain. Blood atonement (the butchering of bodies to save the souls thereof) would have to cease; apostasy could no longer be treated as a capital crime, and no more wealth could be accumulated by the church through the massacre and robbery of passing emigrants. These were "rights" he could not tamely surrender. He would rather sacrifice the last "saint", except himself.

Some months prior to the departure of the Tenth and Fifth regiments of infantry and the two batteries of artillery from the Missouri river for the seat of the rebellion, or as soon as grazing became good on the plains probably as early as the middle of April, 1857 a number of ox trains were loaded at Fort Leavenworth with supplies for the Utah army and started out on their slow march across the plains in order to reach the border of the enemy's country by the time the army caught up. One great freighting firm, Russell, Majors & Waddell, dispatched twelve such trains of their own and several others under sub-contractors. Each of these trains consisted of 26 wagons, with six yokes or 12 oxen to a wagon, four mules, 28 men and two wagon masters, a total of 312 oxen, four mules and thirty men to the train or a grand total of 3244 oxen, 360 men, 312 wagons and 48 mules, besides the men and animals sent out by sub-contractors. The same firm also sent out two or three large droves of beef cattle on foot. One of these (800 head) was captured by the Cheyenne Indians at Plum Creek, near Fort Kearney in Nebraska, after an attack on the camp of the herders in which one of the latter was killed and another severely wounded. These trains were started out early in the spring because they would necessarily make slow progress, from twelve to eighteen miles per day.

Many of these trains reached Utah, on the Big Sandy, Green River, and Ham's Fork, ahead of the Tenth Infantry, the advance regiment of the army, but the Mormons did not molest them until after the army came up. However, a large force of mounted Mormons had threatened some six or seven of these trains packed together on Ham's Fork, guarded by the teamsters and Lieutenant Deshler with a small squad of soldiers left from the escort of Captain Van Vliet on his return from Salt Lake City. Lieutenant Deshler was a brave and determined officer, and had fortified the camp the best he could and worked his own men and the teamsters to the pitch of making a desperate defense; but they would probably have been overpowered and the trains and supplies destroyed by the 400 or 500 Mormons who were coming against them on the morning of September 28th but that the Tenth Infantry marched down the slope to where the trains were parked at 7 A.M. after a forced night march from Green River. That night, however, other mounted Mormons burned one train the army had just passed through, corralled on the divide between Green River and Ham's Fork, another at Green River and a third back on the Big Sandy seventy-five large supply wagons and their contents.

At this time there were no mounted men with or near the army, as Lieutenant Colonel Philip St. George Cooke, who later brought out six companies of his regiment, the Second Dragoons, did not leave

Fort Leavenworth until the 17th of September. For this reason the well-mounted Mormons, who had been hovering about the front, on the flanks and in the rear of the Tenth Infantry from South Pass to Ham's Fork, had things their own way.

The 10th Infantry reached Ham's Fork on the morning of September 28th, the battery of Captain Phelps coming up the next day and the Fifth Infantry and Captain Reno's battery on the 5th of October. Meantime Colonel Alexander had received from Brigham Young the following peremptory order to vacate the territory or surrender his arms;

Governor's Office, Utah Territory
Great Salt Lake City, September 29, 1857.

Sir;

By reference to the act of Congress, passed September 9th, 1850, organizing the Territory of Utah, published in a copy of the Laws of Utah, herewith forwarded, p. 146, Chap. 7, you will find the following;

"Sec. 2. And be it further enacted, That the executive power and authority in and over said Territory of Utah shall be vested in a governor, who shall hold his office for four years, and until his successor shall be appointed and qualified, unless sooner removed by the President of the United States. The Governor shall reside within said Territory, shall be commander-in-chief of the militia thereof," etc. I am still the Governor and Superintendent of Indian affairs for this Territory, no successor having been appointed and qualified, as provided by law, nor have I been removed by the President of the United States.

By virtue of the authority thus vested in me, I have issued and forwarded you a copy of my proclamation, forbidding the entrance of armed forces into this Territory. This you have disregarded. I now further direct that you retire forthwith from the Territory by the same route you entered. Should you deem this impractical, and prefer to remain until spring in the vicinity of your present encampment,

Black's Fork, or Green River, you can do so in peace and unmolested, on condition that you deposit your arms and ammunition with Lewis Robison, Quartermaster General of the Territory, and leave in the spring as soon as the condition of the roads will permit you to march. And should you fall short of provisions, they can be furnished you upon making the proper applications therefor.

General D. H. Wells will forward this and receive any communication you may have to make.

Very respectfully,

Brigham Young,
Governor and Sup't. Indian Affairs, Utah Territory.

To the Officer Commanding the Forces now invading Utah Territory.

Accompanying this was the following note from General Wells, Commander-in-chief of the Mormon forces;

Fort Bridger, September 30, 1857.

Sir;

I have the honor to forward you the accompanying letter from his Excellency Governor Young, together with two copies of his proclamation and a copy of the Laws of Utah, 146, chap. 7, containing the organic act of the Territory.

It may be proper to add, that I am here to aid in carrying out the instructions of Governor Young. General Robison will deliver these papers to you and receive such communication as you may wish to make.

Trusting that your answer and actions will be dictated by a proper respect for the rights and liberties of American citizens,

I am, very respectfully,
Daniel H. Wells.
Lieut. General, Commanding Nauvoo Legion.

Colonel Alexander promptly replied as follows;

Headquarters 10th Regiment Infantry,
Camp Winfield, on Ham's Fork, October 2, 1857.

Sir; I have the honor to acknowledge the receipt of your communication of September 29, 1857, with two copies of proclamation and one of the "Laws of Utah", and have given it an attentive consideration.

I am at present the senior and commanding officer of the troops of the United States at this point, and I will submit your letter to the general commanding as soon as he arrives here.

In the meantime I have only to say, that these troops are here by the orders of the President of the United States, and their future movements and operations will depend entirely upon orders issued by competent military authority.

I am, Sir, very respectfully, & c.
E. B. Alexander,
Col. 10th U.S. Infantry, Commanding.

To Brigham Young, Esq., Governor of Utah Territory.

Upon the arrival at Ham's Fork of the Fifth Infantry and the two batteries of artillery, Colonel Alexander, being the ranking officer, assumed command of the little army on the 5th of October. Of the plan of campaign he determined upon he wrote the adjutant general, October 9th, as follows;

"After much deliberation, and assisted by the counsel of the senior officers, I determined to move the troops by the following route; Up Ham's Fork, about eighteen miles, to a road called Sublette's Cut-off; along that road to Bear River and Soda Spring. On arriving at Soda Spring two routes will be open one down Bear River Valley, towards the Salt Lake, and one to the northeast towards the Wind River Mountains where good valleys for wintering the troops and stock can be found."

Colonel Alexander was under the impression, at that time, that Brevet Colonel C. F. Smith, who was in the rear with 300 men guarding supply trains, and the only force that Colonel Alexander knew of, could join him on Bear River by taking Sublette's Cut off. The army proceeded up Ham's Fork, marching from October 11 to 19, making about thirty-five miles and reaching a point about two miles from the Sublette road, but on the 19th Colonel Alexander ordered a return, having heard from Brevet Colonel Smith, who was so far in the rear, and so much encumbered with supply trains, that it was not likely that he could join him. The Colonel commanding was also actuated in coming to this decision by hearing that Colonel Johnston was assigned to the command and was coming up. So the army retraced its steps down Ham's Fork and went into camp on Black's Fork on the 2nd of November, where, Col. Johnston arrived next day.

Meantime squads of mounted Mormons continued to hover about the army in its movements up and down the valley of Ham's Fork (Colonel Cooke, with the dragoons, being still several hundred miles behind), and occasionally a soldier or teamster who had ventured out in search of game would be picked up and hustled off to Fort Bridger and then to Salt Lake City. The 936 work steers from the three supply trains burned on the road had been driven up to add to the beef supply.

On the 9th of October, two days before starting up Ham's Fork for Sublette's Cut-off, Colonel Alexander, in a report to the adjutant general of the army, wrote;

"The want of cavalry is severely felt; and we are powerless, on account of this deficiency, to effect any chastisement of the marauding bands that are constantly hovering about us".

While the several commands were encamped close together at Camp Winfield, on a low, level, grassy plain on the north bank of Ham's Fork, facing the cliff of a high plateau receding from the south side of the stream, a Captain Smith, who was wagon master with Captain Reno's command, and who had been Captain of the Missouri militia that ran the Mormons out of Jackson County that state (and hence a man who could not expect any mercy from Mormons), accompanied by a teamster named McNeil, crossed the river, ascended the plateau and struck out in search of sage-hens.

They were scarcely out of sight of the army camp when a company of about fifty mounted Mormons, under command of Captain Lot Smith,[##] one of the Destroying Angels, and one of the leaders whom Wagon master Smith had run out of Jackson County, Missouri, dashed in behind them, cut them off and captured them. Wagon master Smith knew that his hide would not hold peas one minute after the Mormons should recognize him, and so he set about making himself as agreeable as possible, in the hope of allaying any suspicion and inducing his captors to relax their vigilance that he might get a chance to escape.

He apparently accepted the situation with great cheerfulness, and at every command or suggestion of the Mormon commander he would reply, with a smile; "Certainly, Captain Smith; at your pleasure," etc. On the contrary, McNeil was sullen and hostile, and cursed his captors soundly for taking him away from his job.

[##] Lot Smith was Captain of one of the four companies of Destroying Angels, or Danites, or Sons of Dan the other three captains being Porter Rockwell, Bill Hickman and Lot Huntington. All four of these Danite Captains bore the closest confidential relations with Brigham Young, although it was understood that only Porter Rockwell and Bill Hickman were entrusted with "private enterprises", such as the assassination of obnoxious individuals, etc. Of all the Mormon Cavalry commanders hovering about the American army in eastern Utah in 1857, Lot Smith was the most active and daring. After the Gentile invasion, following the army, Lot Smith sold out his large farm a few miles north of Salt Lake City and settled in northern Arizona, where he became a Bishop, and where he was shot and killed by Navajo Indians in June, 1892. Smith objected to the Navajoes pasturing their sheep on the public lands near him, and where his cattle grazed, and as they persisted in doing so he killed some of their sheep. The Navajoes retaliated by killing some of his cattle, whereupon Smith opened fire on the Indians and they returned the fire. Smith received a shot in the back, producing a mortal wound, but rode home and died in a few hours.

The Mormon command, with their prisoners, struck straight across the country toward Fort Bridger. They had not gone far until Lot Smith called a halt, and remarked that, owing to the gentlemanly conduct and mild bearing of the elderly wagon master he was satisfied he would never do them any harm, and therefore he would release him; but as the young teamster appeared to be so belligerent and bitter toward them he would take him along.

Captain Smith was not long in making his way back to the army camp and never went out hunting again in that region. McNeil, watched the retreating form until Smith disappeared over the brow of the plateau, then turned upon Lot Smith and said; "Now you have played hell. You take me away from my employment, me who never did any of your people any harm, and turn loose that Captain Smith who commanded the militia that shot down some of your people and drove the rest of you out of Jackson County, Missouri".

Captain Lot Smith was so stunned at the information that he turned deathly pale and gasped for breath, as McNeil said afterward. But it was now too late. The bird had flown. Poor McNeil afterward met the fate that would have been meted out to wagon master Captain Smith had the latter been identified in time. The unfortunate teamster was taken to Salt Lake City and kept in jail until the army entered the valley in the summer of 1858. He then brought suit in the federal court against Brigham Young for $25,000 damages. He was frequently threatened with death if he did not withdraw the suit. When the trial came McNeil was guarded in the courthouse and to and from his meals, in consequence of these threats. When the trial was nearing its end one day, as McNeil was returning through the middle of the street from his dinner to the court house, some shots rang out from the roofs of buildings on each side of the street, and McNeil fell dead between two files of soldiers.

The little army under Colonel Alexander moved southeast and went into camp on Black's Fork of Green River, three miles below the mouth of Ham's Fork, November 2nd, and Colonel Albert Sidney Johnston, the designated commander, came up next day. Having seen the insolent orders and treasonable proclamation of Brigham Young and learned the full extent of Mormon depredation against supply trains, cattle, soldiers and teamsters, on the 5th of November Colonel

Johnston reported to headquarters in the east that in his opinion the time for further argument was past and that the time for prompt and vigorous action had arrived, as the Mormons had, with premeditation," placed themselves in rebellion against the Union, and entertain the insane design of establishing a form of government thoroughly despotic and utterly repugnant to our institution. He had therefore ordered that wherever they were met in arms that they be treated as enemies. In the same report he said that the conduct of the Mormons evidently resulted from a "settled determination on their part not to submit to the authority of the United States or any other outside of their church."

November 6th, 1857, Colonel Johnston commenced his march from the camp three miles below Ham's Fork, up Black's Fork to Camp Scott (Fort Bridger), a distance of thirty-five miles, but so heavy was the snow, so intense the cold and tremendous the loss of battery horses, draught mules and oxen of the contractors that it required fifteen days to cover this distance and it was not an infrequent sight to see old, starved-out, feeble and frozen oxen drop dead under the yoke, while endeavoring to drag heavy freight wagons through the snow.

Lieutenant Colonel Philip St. George Cooke, with six companies of the Second Dragoons, reached winter quarters at Fort Bridger November 19th, after the loss by hunger and cold, of 134 horses out of 278, and much suffering among the men during the fifteen days of heavy snows and intense cold, which seems to have prevailed throughout the Rocky Mountain range from Arctic regions to New Mexico.

These six companies of dragoons had just returned from a campaign of 600 miles over the plains, when Lieutenant Colonel Philip St. George Cooke hurriedly reorganized them and started out from Fort Leavenworth on the 17th of September. The mules furnished him for transportation purposes were also well worn down by a continuous tramp of 2,000 miles to Bridger's Pass and back. He encountered heavy rain on the fifth day out, and from then to the 12th of October inclusive, rain poured down continuously, increasing the pull on his team mules and at the same time steadily diminishing their strength. Feed was also scarce and this trouble steadily increased along the whole route.

On the 17th of October snow and sleet began to fall, the weather became intensely cold and horses and mules began to die off rapidly.

At Fort Laramie he was compelled to drop fifty-three dragoon horses as ineffective, ten supply wagons and their teams, all the laundresses and sick, and all others deemed "ineffective a-foot." On account of the intense cold all horses were kept blanketed at night, and on the march were led and mounted, alternate hours, and were led over all difficult ground.

At the last crossing of the North Platte five wagons, and teams of worst mules, were left in camp to be returned to Fort Laramie, and from Sweetwater, November, 4th, five more wagons and teams were ordered back.

At Bitter Creek November 8th, after a three days' tramp through deep snow and a freezing, blinding fog, twenty-three mules gave out and five wagons and their harness were abandoned.

On the night of the 9th fifteen animals froze to death, and on account of the bitter cold wind facing them and the frozen fog in their faces none of the loose animals could be forced out of the dead brush in the valley that afforded them scant shelter, and that night three-fourths of those remaining perished from the cold. The same day nine-trooper horses were left freezing and dying on the road.

On the night of the 10th the mercury went 25° below zero, and on the morning of the 11th, fifty mules having perished in thirty-six hours, three wagons were abandoned, two of them empty and the other hidden in the brush and filled with 74 extra saddles and bridles and some sabers.

On the 11th the command went through the South Pass, 9,000 feet above sea level, and the weather was intensely cold. That night the mules were tied to the wagons, where nine of them perished, while the others gnawed and destroyed four wagon tongues, a number of wagon covers, ate their ropes, and, getting loose, ate the sage brush fuel collected at the tents, and attacked the tents.

From the loss of horses more than half of the men were now dismounted, and on the morning of November 12th a number were frost-bitten while standing by camp fires. The sick report had rapidly run up from four or five to forty-two to thirty-six soldiers and teamsters having been frosted.

November 15th Green River was reached and crossed on the ice, and on the 16th nine wagons and forty-two mules were left there, twenty horses having also been abandoned in twenty-four hours.

On reaching General Johnston's headquarters Lieutenant Colonel Cooke made a detailed report of his trip, concluding as follows;

"I have 144 horses and have lost 134. Most of the loss has occurred, much this side of South Pass, in comparatively moderate weather. It has been of starvation. The earth has a no more lifeless, treeless, grassless desert; It contains scarcely a wolf to glut itself on the hundreds of dead and frozen animals, which for thirty miles nearly block the road, with abandoned and shattered property. They mark, perhaps beyond example in history, the steps of an advancing army, with the horrors of a disastrous retreat."

As might have been expected, when the rigorous weather of this elevated and inhospitable region began to cast the shadow of death over better men and all inferior animals, the Mormons, whose recalcitrant fanaticism had caused all this suffering, retired into the warm valleys behind their formidable fortifications in Echo Canon, leaving only a few squads to watch the mountain passes and the movement (if any) of the army and to shoot down, without a word of warning, any and all apostates who might attempt to escape the reign of terror in the cities and valleys of the territory and find protection with the American army. These squads were relieved at short intervals and allowed to retire to the city of the saints to rest and recuperate, and to be lionized.

The winter of 1857-8 was an unusually severe one, even for that region of severe winters, and the snow-fall was uncommonly heavy. Of coarse in the deep, warm valley of Salt Lake City there was very little if any snow the precipitation being in the form of gentle showers of rain. In the early part of the winter, when the snow began to whiten only the loftiest peaks and ridges, and then to creep down the sides of the mountains and melt into rain below the freezing zone, the Mormon apostles and elders, preaching in the Tabernacle, every Sunday would "point with pride" to the eastern mountains and call the attention of the people to the "fact" that the Lord was punishing the "Gentile army" with heavy snows and blockading the mountain passes against their approach, while at the same time He was sending to the Saints warm, gentle rains to fructify their soil. No Mormon seemed to question that this single occurrence, that may be viewed every winter in every mountainous region where snow falls, was anything short of a direct, visible and tangible interference in their favor on the part of Heaven so simple and credulous were these ignorant zealots.

So great had been the loss of cavalry and battery horses and draught mules that General Johnston foresaw that he would be unable to move his army the following spring even after the snow had disappeared, so on the 24th of November, 1857, he ordered Captain Randolph B. Marcy of the Fifth Infantry to proceed, "across lots" and through the heart of the Uintah, Henry and Rocky Mountains to the department of New Mexico to procure additional animals, and to return with them as early as possible the following spring. Captain Marcy set out on the 27th armed with a letter from General Johnston to General Garland, commander of the department of New Mexico, stating that a large proportion of cavalry and battery horses, as well as many draught animals of the command, had been starved by the unprecedented cold weather of the last month and the great scarcity of grass, and that he had ordered Capt. Marcy to proceed to New Mexico to purchase a remount for the dragoons and batteries and a sufficient number of draught animals to replace those which had died or been broken down on the march. He also requested that a sufficient escort be provided for the return trip. Of this perilous trip and the patient heroism and terrible sufferings of the men under his command, Captain Marcy gave a very graphic report on his return to Fort Bridger, June 12th, 1858. He took with him an escort of forty soldiers, volunteers from the Fifth and Tenth regiments of infantry, and twenty-four citizens as guides, packers and herders. The expedition started on the 27th of November 1857, after the severe winter of that year was well on, and the first building to be encountered on the route was at Fort Massachusetts 593 miles distant. This post has since been moved down a few miles to the mouth of the canyon at the foot of Wet Mountain, Colorado, and called Fort Garland.

The route followed was southerly, with dim and in many places indistinguishable Indian trails, through the deep gorges of Henry's Fork, Green River, White River, Box Elder Creek, Grand River, the Bunkaree, Compadre and other tributaries of the Colorado of the West, and over many of the loftiest plateaux, water sheds and culminant peaks of the Wasatch, Uintah, Henry and Rocky Mountain ranges.

On the 3rd of December, in crossing the elevated plateau dividing the waters of Green and Grand Rivers, they encountered two feet of snow, all feed for animals had disappeared and the poor horses and mules began to fail and several were abandoned.

In descending the precipitous side of the escarpment to Grand River, for probably 1,800 feet, several of the weakened pack mules lost their footing and rolled thirty or forty feet down the bluff before being stopped by a projecting tree or rock.

In ascending the Compadre several lodges of Utah Indians were encountered, and Captain Marcy tried in vain to purchase fresh horses from them. He also tried in vain to hire one of the Indians as guide to the Kutch-e-tope pass, thinking the Indian would know the best route to avoid deep snow, and offered him the price of two horses to go, but the Indian peremptorily declined, saying the snow was very deep in the mountains, that they would all perish, and that for his part he was not disposed to die that way.

On the 22nd of December the expedition left the valley of the Compadre and struck into the mountains, where they encountered deep snow bearing a heavy crust of ice, which cut the mules' legs severely and completely obscured all grass. Here every article of baggage that could possibly be dispensed with was abandoned.

From the 24th to the 27th inclusive the snow was so deep that Captain Marcy put forty men ahead to break a trail, alternating from front to rear as they became exhausted, and over this trail the pack mules with difficulty passed and thirteen more of them were abandoned.

Finding his means of subsistence so rapidly diminishing and the snow still increasing in depth, on the morning of December 28th Captain Marcy dispatched two Mexicans, with three of his best remaining animals, with a letter to the commanding officer at Fort

Massachusetts informing him of the situation and requesting him to send supplies.

This heroic little party continued to struggle on thus until the 10th of January, making from two to five miles per day through the deep snow, which was being almost daily increased in depth by snow storms, and for the last ten days of this time they were compelled to subsist solely upon the carcasses of their starved out mules. "Yet these noble hearts of oak never for a moment faltered or uttered a murmur of discouragement or insubordination," adds Captain Marcy in his report.

Supplies reached them on the 12th, and on the 18th of January they reached Fort Massachusetts, where they were hospitably entertained by Captain W. W. Bowman of the Third Infantry. They then proceeded to Taos, N.M. and after seeing his escort comfortably quartered Captain Marcy proceeded to the purchase of animals, and by the 13th of March he had 960 mules and 160 horses assembled at Rayedo, the extreme border settlement upon his return route.

On the 17th of March 1858, he started on his return to Utah, taking the Leavenworth road over the Raton Mountains to Purgatoire creek and thence in a northwest course to the Old Pueblo on the Arkansas River. On the return trip nothing unusual occurred, except that on the night of April 29th, while the party was encamped on the ridge dividing the waters of the Arkansas from those of the Platte, a snow-storm came on with a violent tempest of wind, and raged with unabated fury for sixty hours. Three hundred horses and mules broke away, in spite of the efforts of the herders, and ran directly with the wind for fifty miles. Of two Mexicans who followed one was afterward found frozen to death and the other crawling upon his hands and knees in a state of temporary insanity. Another man perished within two hundred yards of the camp. Nearly all of the stampeded animals were recovered after the storm, and the expedition proceeded on to Fort Bridger, distant from Rayedo 741 miles.

Secretary of war John F. Floyd, in his annual report for 1858, said of Captain Marcy's expedition; "It may be safely affirmed that in the whole catalogue of hazardous expeditions, scattered so thickly through the history of our border warfare, filled as many of them with appalling tales of privation, hardship and suffering, not one surpasses this and in some particulars it has been hardly equaled by any."

While all this suffering of men and animals, and all this enormous expense to the government and people was being entailed east of the Wasatch range of mountains in consequence of the Mormon rebellion, Brigham Young and his apostles were comfortably situated in their homes in the city, and every Sunday in the Tabernacle they were hurling anathemas at the army, the government and the people of the United States, bidding defiance to the authority of the government, and actually making many of their ignorant followers believe that they would individually be invulnerable to the fire of a whole regiment of soldiers as "the Lord would turn aside any and all bullets that might be fired at them". Brigham himself, however, did not believe his own bombast, for while he was preaching it to his deluded followers every Sunday, during the week he was busily and very earnestly engaged in his office in his Lion mansion in patching up a peace with the commissioners to be sent out that winter by the President for that purpose. Brigham and his friends in Washington urged President Buchanan to appoint such a commission and send them out, so as to reach there in time to save him from the consequences of his many and heinous crimes when the disappearance of the snow would enable the army to force its way into the valley in the spring. To show how extremely anxious Brigham was to settle the affair and surrender before the army got within range of himself or his military forces, even after all his bombast, it is only necessary to state, in advance of its regular order, that on the 21st of the following May, seventeen days in advance of the arrival of the commissioners, and thirty-six days in advance of the arrival of the army in the city, Brigham had called in his army and had himself unconditionally surrendered to Governor Cumming alone.

Among other extraordinary expenses necessarily incurred by the government in this campaign, Captain J. H. Dickerson, Quartermaster General to the Army of Utah, to prevent heavy reclamations on the government for loss by reason of appropriation of private property, entered into a contract with James Bridger for the lease of the tract of land on which Fort Bridger was situated, for ten years at $600 per year. As there was some doubt as to the validity of Bridger's title to the land, the contract was so drawn that no payment was to be made until Bridger should establish his title.

Meantime, moreover, Brigham Young and other beneficiaries of the Mormon Church were accumulating large sums of money and other valuable property by the massacre of emigrants and other American citizens attempting to pass through the territory after martial law was proclaimed. It was for the purpose of throwing a shadow of the shield of legality over these atrocious butcheries, and for the additional purpose of preventing many of his own people from deserting him rather than come into armed conflict with the government, that that "grim and bloody monster" declared martial law.

The Mountain Meadows massacre had already been decreed, but was carried out four days before martial law was proclaimed in the city 283 miles distant. And there were no telegraph lines in Utah at that time. The Aiken party of six Californians were assassinated in camp at the crossing of Sevier river two or three weeks later. There was no pretense nor contention that these men were killed by Indians. But they had sixteen fine animals, good arms and outfit, and $18,000 in United States gold coin; other assassinations chiefly of Mormons accused of apostasy were of almost daily occurrence during the fall and winter of 1857.

Superstition had banished reason and humanity utterly. Men who, under ordinary circumstances, and free from brutalizing superstition would have been at least as sympathetic toward their own species as were the untutored animals of the lower orders, became fiends incarnate. That men can and do become so completely transformed by a mere sentiment or belief has been the marvel of thinkers for centuries.

Under the common sense laws enacted by intelligent legislators everywhere, no witness in a court of justice is allowed to testify as to what he believes, he is confined strictly to what he *knows.* Under the lax latitude of superstition, knowledge and reason are subordinated wholly to belief by faith, however flimsy may be the foundation of that faith, and however audacious the pretense of the interested priesthood who promulgate it. The very motto of science, which is human wisdom in its essence, is that "well ascertained facts, experimentally proven, are alone sacred and lasting". Superstition, which is defined by lexicographers as "excessive credulity", requires no proof; in fact will not listen to any testimony offered, but swallows with avidity and relish, the most absurd and ridiculous mouthings of the beneficiaries of their credulity.

Hence the perversion and transformation of human nature. The rattlesnake, in his most apprehensive and angry mood in dog days, is a more desirable and genial companion.

The 136 men, women and children so mercilessly shot down at Mountain Meadows, after they had surrendered their arms to their fellow countrymen and fellow Christians under promise of protection back to Cedar City (about 45 miles), were known in crossing the plains as the Perkins party, a man named Perkins, who had previously been to California, being the conductor or captain. There were about forty families in the party all wealthy or well-to-do people, chiefly farmers, and, beside a large number of fine cattle, horses and mules, it was estimated that they had in the aggregate at least $90,000 in money. After the massacre all this booty went to the Mormon Church or its authorities. In the spring of 1859, twenty months after the slaughter, Brevet Major James Henry Carleton, then Captain the First Dragoons and afterward a General in the Civil Way, was ordered from California to the Mountain Meadows to inquire into the facts of the massacre and bury the bones of the men, women and children slaughtered. Major Carleton arrived on the ground May 16th, 1859, encamped on the spot where the murdered emigrants were encamped when first attacked, and after as full investigation as it was possible to make there and then, wrote out his report on the 25th of May.

Dr. Brewer, U.S. Army, whom Major Carleton met with Captain Reuben P. Campbell's command on the Santa Clara, informed Major Carleton that he (Dr. Brewer) visited the Perkins party several times during the month of June, 1857, as the party was ascending the North Platte river; that he noticed particularly a peculiar carriage in which some ladies rode; there was something peculiar in the construction of the carriage and its ornaments, its blazoned stag's head on the panels, etc. After the massacre (and recently) he had seen this carriage in the possession of the Mormons. The party had about forty wagons and some tents, about forty heads of families, many women, some unmarried, and many children, probably 136 persons in all, highly respectable and well to do people from Arkansas. Major Carleton estimated the number slaughtered at 120, seventeen children being saved.

Jacob Hamblin, a cattleman claiming the Mountain Meadows and residing at the north end of the same, about five miles from the spring where the emigrants were first attacked, a zealous and obedient Mormon, an Indian interpreter and guide for emigrants, and sub-agent at the time of the massacre for the southern Piute Indians (appointed by Brigham Young) gave Major Carleton about the same false testimony touching the matter of the massacre as he had previously given to U.S. Judge Cradlebaugh and for the same reason; to allay suspicion against the real murderers (the Mormons) and to relieve them from the consequences of a more searching inquiry. This testimony of Hamblin, and that of his oldest wife, given to Major Carleton in Hamblin's presence and prompted by him from time to time, is a tissue of falsehoods from beginning to end, as was plain to five Americans who passed over the ground three weeks after the massacre and soon afterward consulted with a large party of Texans for whom Hamblin was acting guide in the vicinity on the very day of the massacre. Besides, Hamblin had about 100 head of the emigrants' cattle on his ranch, and kept them until relatives or friends of the murdered emigrants came along the next year and demanded them, when Hamblin gave them up.

The elder Mrs. Hamblin admitted hearing the firing at the emigrant camp from time to time from Monday morning early until Friday evening after sunset, and that about an hour after the last shots were fired a wagon containing seventeen little children was driven up to her house by a man named Schurtz or Shirts, a son-in-law of John D. Lee. Some of these little ones had been wounded, the clothing of some were, dripping with the blood of their murdered mothers or sisters, and all were terror-stricken and crying. Bishop John D. Lee, who had commanded the Mormons during the siege and massacre, seemed to have the distributing of the children. One, a girl about a year old had been shot through the arm, rendering the limb useless for life, and another had been wounded in the ear. The mangled baby could not well be carried on to Cedar City, nearly forty miles, and as she had two sisters, Rebecca, aged seven, and Louisa, aged five years, Mrs. Hamblin persuaded Lee to let her keep all three of them, as they were devotedly attached to each other. This he finally agreed to do, and Mrs. Hamblin nursed the wounded baby back to life, through it never recovered the use of the wounded arm, as a considerable portion of bone had been carried away by a large ball. The next day the Mormons returned to Cedar City with the other orphaned children and the property of the murdered emigrants.

A young Snake Indian named Albert, who had belonged to Hamblin for many years, and who spoke English fluently, was also sent to Major Carleton's camp to confirm the stories of Hamblin and wife. Hamblin who was a shrewd diplomat by nature and an ardent Mormon ever ready to resort to the most shocking atrocity to further the ends of the beneficiaries of his blind faith, evidently prepared these stories and rehearsed them in his "family" frequently in order to be fully prepared for any court of inquiry that might come along. Albert, however, on being questioned, admitted seeing a good many leading Mormons from Cedar City, Harmony, Pinto Creek, "and about", passing to and fro and stopping at Hamblin's house while the emigrants were being besieged naming John D. Lee, Richard Robinson, Prime Coleman, Amos Thornton and Brother Dickinson.

Hamblin's story was to the effect that the Pah Utah Indians of the south had killed the emigrants because the latter poisoned a spring near the Corn Creek farms of the Parovan Indians, 151 miles north of the Mountains Meadows. A similar story prevailed in Salt Lake City 148 miles still further north with this material difference; The Salt Lake City story was to the effect that the Parovan Indians had followed the emigrants to Mountain Meadows and killed them, because the latter had poisoned a spring at Corn Creek. This the Parovans could have done as they could muster 400 warriors all armed with guns but they did not follow these emigrants a single mile, and never heard of the spring poisoning until it reached them from Salt Lake City.

U.S. Deputy Marshal Roberts, who accompanied Judge Cradlebaugh on his southern tour, told Major Carleton that "the water of the spring referred to runs with such volume and force a barrel of arsenic would not poison it."

In summing up, Major Carleton said he thought the following account of the affair was susceptible of legal proof by those whose names were known and who, he was assured, were willing to make oath of the facts which would serve as links in the chain of evidence leading toward the truth as to who murdered these 120 men, women and children;

"It was currently reported among the Mormons at Cedar City, in talking among themselves, before the troops ever came down south (when all felt secure from arrest or prosecution), and nobody seemed to question the truth of it, that a train of emigrants of fifty or more men, mostly with families came and encamped at this spring at Mountain Meadows in September, 1857. It was reported in Cedar City, and was not, and is not doubted even by the Mormons that John D. Lee, Isaac C. Haight, John M. Higby (the first resides at Harmony, the last two at Cedar City), were the leaders who organized a party of fifty or sixty Mormons to attack this train.

"They had also all the Indians which they could collect at Cedar City, Harmony, and Washington City to help them, a good many in number. This party then came down, and at first the Indians were ordered to stampede the cattle to drive them away from the train. They then commenced firing on the emigrants; this firing was returned by the emigrants; one Indian was killed, a brother of the chief of the Santa Clara Indians, another shot through the leg, who is now a cripple at Cedar City. There were without doubt a great many more killed or wounded. It was said the Mormons were painted and disguised as Indians. The Mormons say the emigrants fought "like lions," and that they saw they could not whip them by any fair fighting.

"After some days fighting the Mormons had a council among themselves to arrange a plan to destroy the emigrants. They concluded, finally, that they would send some few down and pretend to be friends and try and get the emigrants to surrender. John D. Lee and three or four others, headmen, from Washington, Cedar and Parowan (Haight, and Higby from Cedar), had their paint washed off and, dressing in their usual dress, took their wagons and drove toward the emigrant's corral as if they were just traveling on the road on their ordinary business. The emigrants sent out a little girl toward them.

She was dressed in white and had a white handkerchief in her hand, which she waved in token of peace. The Mormons with the wagons waved one in reply, and then moved on to the corral. The emigrants them came out, no Indians or others being in sight at this time, and talked with these leading Mormons with the three wagons.

"They talked with the emigrants an hour or an hour and a half, and told them that the Indians were hostile, and that if they gave up their arms it would show that they did not want to fight; and if they, the emigrants, would do this they would pilot them back to the settlements. The emigrants had horses, which had remained near their wagons; the loose stock, mostly cattle, had been driven off, not the horses. Finally the emigrants agreed to these terms and delivered up their arms to the Mormons with whom they had counseled. The women and children then started back toward Hamblin's house, the men following with a few wagons that they had hitched up. On arriving at the Scrub Oaks, etc., where the other Mormons and Indians lay concealed, Higby, who had been one of those who had inveigled the emigrants from their defenses, himself gave the signal to fire, when a volley was poured in from each side, and the butchery commenced.

"The property was brought to Cedar City and sold at public auction. It was called in Cedar City, and is so called now by the facetious Mormons," property taken at the siege of Sebastopol". The clothing stripped from the corpses, bloody and with bits of flesh in it, shredded by the bullets from the persons of the poor creatures who wore it, was placed in the cellar of the tithing office (an official building), where it lay about three weeks, when it was brought away by some of the party; but witnesses do not know whether it was sold or given away. It is said the cellar smells even to this day."

General Carleton further reported that the seventeen little children saved from the massacre, ten girls and seven boys, ranging in age from three to nine years (in 1859), were subsequently gathered up from among the Mormons of southern Utah by Dr. Forney, Gentile Indian agent, and restored to relatives and friends in Arkansas. Sixteen of these were seen by Judge Cradlebaugh, Lieutenant Kearney and others, and gave the following information in relation to their identity;

"The first is a boy named Calvin, between 7 and 8; does not remember his surname; says he was by his mother when she was killed, and pulled the arrows from her back until she was dead; says he had two brothers older than himself, named Henry and James, and three sisters, Nancy, Mary and Martha.

"The second is a girl, who does not remember her name. The others say it is Demurr.

"The Third is a boy named Ambrose Miriam Tagit; says he had two brothers older than himself and one younger. His father, mother, and two elder brothers were killed, his younger brother was brought to Cedar City; says he lives in Johnson county, but does not know what State; says it took one week to go from where he lived to his grandfather's and grandmother's, who are still living in the States.

"The fourth is a girl obtained of John Morris, a Mormon, at Cedar City. She does not recollect anything about herself.

"Fifth. A boy obtained of E. F. Grove, says that the girl obtained of Morris is named Mary and is his sister.

"The sixth is a girl who says her name is Prudence Angelina. Had two brothers, Jessee and John, who were killed. Her father's name was Williams, and she had an uncle Jesses.

"The seventh is a girl. She says her name is Francis Harris, or Horne; remembers nothing of her family.

"The eighth is a young boy; too young to remember anything about himself.

"The ninth is a boy who says his name is William W. Huff.

"The tenth is a boy who says his name is Charles Francher.

"The eleventh is a girl who says her name is Sophronia Huff.

"The twelfth is a girl who says her name is Betsey.

"The thirteenth, fourteenth, and fifteenth are three sisters named Rebecca, Louisa, and Sarah Dunlap. These three sisters were the children obtained of Jacob Hamblin."

No note of the sixteenth.

"The seventeenth was a boy who was but six weeks old at the time of the massacre. Hamblin's wife took him to Major Carleton's camp on the 19th May 1859. The next day they took him on to Salt Lake City to give him up to Dr. Forney. He was a pretty little boy, and hardly dreamed he had again slept upon the ground where his parents had been murdered.

These children, it is said, could not be induced to make any developments while they remained with the Mormons, from fear, no doubt, having been intimidated by threats. Dr. Forney, it is said, went southward for them under the impression that he would find them in the hands of the Indians. The Mormons said the children were in the hands of the Indians and were purchased by themselves for rifles, blankets, etc., but the children said they had never lived with the Indians at all. The Mormons claimed of Dr. Forney sums of money, varying from $200 to $400, for attending them when sick, for feeding and clothing them, and for nourishing the infants from the time when they assumed to have purchased them from the Indians. On this subject Major Carleton wrote;

"Murderers of the parents and despoilers of their property, these Mormons, rather these relentless, incarnate fiends dared even to come forward and claim payment for having kept these little ones barely alive, these helpless orphans whom they themselves had already robbed of their natural protectors and support. Has there ever been an act, which at all equaled this devilish hardihood, in more than devilish effrontery? Never, but one; and even then the price was but 30 pieces of silver."

Major Carleton gathered up skeletons and fragments of skeletons over an area of several square miles and buried them in one grave on the northern side of the ditch dug by the murdered emigrants when they were first attacked. Over this he erected a monument of loose granite stones conical in form, fifty feet in circumference at the base and twelve feet in height, surmounted by a cross, twelve feet higher, hewn from red cedar wood. On the transverse of the cross, facing towards the north (and Mormondom) this inscription was carved deeply in the wood;

"Vengeance is mine; I will repay, saith the Lord." And on a rude slab of granite, set in the earth and leaning against the northern base of the monument, there are cut the following words;

"Here 120 men, women and children were massacred in cold blood early in September, 1857. They were from Arkansas".

But one man is known to have escaped from the beleaguered emigrant camp, and he was pursued by Ira Hatch, Prime Coleman and two other Mormons named Young, all of whom doubtless participated in the massacre, more than 100 miles, beyond the Muddy, where he was wandering about, wounded, nearly starved and in a demented condition. His throat was promptly cut and he was buried in the sand.

All the money, family carriages, wagons, live stock (including 900 head of fine cattle), arms, clothing, household goods and other property taken from the murdered emigrants was taken back to Cedar City by the Mormon murderers.

The white Mormons made the distinction between themselves and all others as Mormons and Gentiles, but the Indian Mormons (and all the Utah's, Pah Utah's, Pah Vents, Piedes and Parovans in the territory, had been converted to Mormonism and become completely subject to the church authorities prior to 1857) distinguished between Mormons and all others by calling one "Mormony" and the other "Mericat" (meaning American). A Chinaman or a full-blooded African was either Mormony or "Mericat. As the distinction could not be made with certainty by the color or appearance of a person, the Mormons had introduced a secret grip among the Indians, by which the latter could tell, with certainty, after shaking hands, however much a person might protest that he was a Mormony. It was the habit of all these Mormon Indians, on approaching a stranger, to inquire; "Mormony or 'Mericat?" In those hostile days nearly every American would naturally reply; "Mormony". Where upon the Indian would approach and shake hands, with his usual greeting "How?" If he failed to receive the Mormon grip he would step back, point his finger at the pretender, and, with an expression of mingled pity and contempt upon his countence, assert most positively; "No Mormony".

However, this amity and fraternity between the Mormons and Indians had not always existed. When the Mormons first settled in Utah in 1847 the Indians made war upon them, just as other wild tribes had warred against other whites who had intruded upon the country claimed by the reds, and this war was kept up for four years. As the settlements extended down through the valleys southward from

Salt Lake, each town or village was walled in and otherwise fortified to resist the attacks of the Indians, and while the men folks, with their fire arms, were working on the farms outside, the women folks frequently had to defend their homes in the village. Soon apostles, bishops and elders of the church began marrying squaws to enlarge their harems, and, as all wild Indians are naturally polygamous, it required but a few years to convert all the Indians of the territory to the Mormon church. In order to cement more closely the friendship and fraternity of the two races the language of the Indians was reduced to writing and taught in the Mormon schools. Influential chieftains, like Kanosh of the powerful Paravan tribe, were made elders of the church, and by these and other stratagems the two races were brought into the closest communion of which fraternal fanaticism is capable. This also added greatly to Brother Brigham's military strength whenever he should choose to defy the government.

If an American was clad in well-worn clothing, with long and unkept hair, and was particularly dirty (as was often the case after a long trip across the plains), he could very readily pass himself off upon the Indians as a Mormon only so long as he could avoid shaking hands with any of them. The first party of Americans or Gentiles known to have passed over the ground after the massacre at Mountain Meadows consisted of seven men, besides four or five Mormons who furnished them with transportation from Salt Lake City to San Bernardino, California. Although five of the seven were young at that time, some of these men were keen and trained observers, and made diligent inquiries about the massacre, both from white and Indian Mormons, all the way from Salt Lake City until they passed out of the Indian country, 450 miles to the southwest. They passed over the scene of the massacre about three weeks after the butchery, and while the bodies of the men women and children butchered were still in a state of almost perfect preservation. From all they could learn, by inquiry and observation, they were forced to the conclusion that the Mormons alone and the very heads of the church themselves were responsible for that most atrocious and cowardly crime.

They came to the conclusion, also, that the "Siege of Sebastopol" as the Mormons facetiously called the process by which the Indians (acting under the written orders of Brigham Young) held the doomed emigrants in camp until the Mormon militia could get there with guns to kill them, was begun on Monday, September 7th, 1857, and continued until the following Friday, September 11th when Major John D. Lee, the Mormon commander, Isaac C. Haight, and John M. Higby, finding they could not slaughter these people with safety while they had arms in their hands, entered their fortified camp under a flag of truce and prevailed upon them to surrender their arms, "just to appease the Indians", and under the solemn promise from Lee and his associates that they would protect the emigrants in safety back to Cedar City.

Thus disarmed, these men, with many delicate women and children who were not permitted to ride even in their own wagons or family carriages, were started in procession on the road back toward Cedar City. They had proceeded about one mile when John M. Higby, one of the Mormon leaders who had induced them to surrender their arms, gave the signal and the doomed emigrants were fired upon by their Mormon captors from both sides of the line, and something more than one-third of their number fell.

Just why the slaughter ceased at this stage has never been certainly known, though years afterward Mormons, who claimed to have been on the ground at the time, explained that the Mormon militiamen themselves revolted at the thought and sight of slaughtering innocent and defenseless women and children, and ceased to fire.

This was probably the case. At any rate, the scene disclosed the fact that the remainder of the doomed emigrants were marched more than one mile further back toward Cedar City and there shot down.

It will be seen by his testimony before Major Carleton (which was a palpable "whitewash" of the Mormons) that Jake Hamblin said he got to his home at the north end of the Mountain Meadows on the 18th of September exactly one week after the emigrants were killed. But instead of reaching home on that date from the north, as he says, he doubtless reached there from the south where he had gone to conduct a strong Texas train (which he took off of the road and around the scene of the massacre of the very day it occurred) as far south as the Muddy, about 100 miles. It would have taken him just about one week to go to the Muddy with the Texas train and return by saddle or buggy. That he took this Texas train off from a good road and out through the woods and over mountains where they had to let their wagons down by taking a hitch around a tree by strong ropes, to keep this strong and well armed party of Texans from any knowledge of the desperate condition of the Perkins or (Fancher) party, is conclusive proof that Jake Hamblin had foreknowledge of what was to occur on the Mountain Meadows that day.

But for this misguidance of the Texas train possibly ordered by Major John D. Lee, commander of the Mormon militia engaged in the slaughter, though more likely initiated by Hamblin himself to facilitate the massacre of which he had foreknowledge at any rate, but for this stratagem the Texas train would probably have slaughtered or routed both the Mormon militia and the few Indians present and have taken the Perkins or (Fancher) party through to California in safety. Unfortunately for these victims of "prophecy" however, the co-operation of the Mormons was too perfect.

Subsequent events transpiring in Utah, during the winter of 1857-8 and the spring and summer of the latter year, were equally interesting though not so tragic and sanguinary. While the American Army was confined in winter quarters at Fort Bridger by deep snow and a shortage of animals and with the great intervening mountain gorges of Echo Canyon and Weber river choked with snow and strongly fortified, the Mormons remained sullen and defiant. They had not only "proclaimed martial law in that territory without a pretext, and against every principle of justice, of law, and of the constitution," (as well said by the Secretary of War) but had "embodied their whole force of effective men and kept them constantly drilled and under arms." They had also sent numerous emissaries among the five Indian tribes of Washington Territory and the powerful Navajo tribe of northern Arizona and western New Mexico to incite them to hostilities against the government hoping thus to divert the little army away from themselves or at least of diverting any or all reinforcements away from Johnston's army. Thus matters stood until early in the spring of 1858, when large reinforcements were started from Fort Leavenworth for Fort Bridger, when Mormon bluster and bravado sank into whispers of terror and submission.

On the 4th of January, 1858, General Johnston wrote to army headquarters from Fort Bridger that a soldier who had been hospital steward with the Tenth Infantry and had been captured by the Mormons early in the preceding October, had been released and had returned to his regiment, with the report that the Mormons were organizing four companies of mounted men to go out and stampede or capture the horses and mules it was expected Captain Marcy would bring out in the spring from New Mexico. Both General Johnston and General Scott, commander-in-chief, at once notified General Garland, commander of the department of New Mexico, of this contemplated raid, and requested that a strong escort be provided for Captain Marcy. Col. W. W. Loring, of the Mounted Rifle regiment then in New Mexico, was detailed with 346 mounted riflemen to accompany the 162 men of Captain Marcy's party to Fort Bridger. This brought the force up to 508 men, and the Mormons never made any further attempt to disturb them.

General Johnston, who took command of the army for Utah with the rank of Colonel of the Second Cavalry, was brevetted Brigadier General about the first of May 1858. During the autumn and winter preceding he had witnessed so much loss and suffering that he was "full of fight" and was anxious for a conflict at arms that he might inflict deserved punishment upon those who had caused so much suffering and expense. On the 20th of January 1858, he wrote to the headquarters of the army;

"Knowing how repugnant it would be to the policy or interest of the government to do any act that would force these people into unpleasant relations with the federal government, I would, in conformity with the views also of the commanding general, on all proper occasions have manifested in intercourse with them a spirit of conciliation, but I do not believe that such consideration for them would be properly appreciated now, or rather would be wrongly interpreted; in view of the treasonable temper and feeling now pervading the leaders and a greater portion of the Mormons, I think that neither the honor nor the dignity of the government will allow of the slightest concession being made to them."

General Johnston added that the Mormon threat to oppose the march of the troops in the spring would not have the slightest influence in delaying it; that he thought they should be made to submit to the demands of the government unconditionally, and if they desired to join issue, he believed it was for the interest of the government that they should have the opportunity.

Colonel Thomas L. Kane, of Philadelphia, a devoted friend to Brigham Young and the Mormon people, and a gentlemen possessing the confidence and esteem of President Buchanan, appears to have been the first person to suggest to the President the propriety of sending one or more peace commissioners to Utah to patch up a peace with Brigham Young before the army could get a whack at him. Whether Colonel Kane applied to the President to have himself appointed as such commissioner is not certainly known, but it would appear from two letters from President Buchanana to Colonel Kane that he did. Each of these letters bore date December 31st, 1857, the first expressing the greatest esteem for Colonel Kane and Mr. Buchanan's admiration for his disinterested devotion to peace in going to Utah in the dead of winter at his own expense and as a private citizen, and the other commending him to the good offices of the military officers at the front. The next heard of Colonel Kane was from a letter written by Governor Cumming to General Johnston, dated Great Salt Lake City, April 15th, 1858, in which the new Governor says he left Fort Bridger for the city on the 5th of April with Colonel Kane as his guide. Subsequently Colonel Kane vibrated between the city and General Johnston's headquarters quite often, carrying on considerable correspondence of a concilitary nature at both ends of the line. Doubtless, however, Colonel Kane had been in Great Salt Lake City for some time prior to the 5th of April, or at least it is known that he was in close communication with Brigham Young prior to that date, and he doubtless paved the way for the entrance of Governor Cumming not only into the city but upon the duties of his office.

The civil officers appointed for Utah, and who spent the winter of 1857-8 with General Johnston's army at Fort Bridger, Green river county, Utah, were; Alfred Cumming, Governor; John Hartnett, Secretary D. H. Eckels, Chief Justice of the Supreme Court; P. K. Dotson, Marshal; Dr. J. Forney, Superintendent of Indian Affairs, and

Dr. Garland Hurt, Indian Agent. The associate justices of the Supreme Court did not get out to Utah until the summer of 1858.

Notwithstanding President Buchanan's declaration to Colonel Kane that he would not at that moment (December 31st, 1857), "in view of the hostile attitude they (the Mormons) have assumed against the United States, send any agent to visit them on behalf of the government," for some reason or other he changed his mind three months afterward, for on the 12th of April, 1858, the Secretary of War issued under the seal of the Department of War, a certificate to the effect that "Lazarus W. Powell, of Kentucky, and Ben McCulloch, of Texas, have been authorized by the President to proceed to Utah to perform certain duties more particularly set forth in instructions of this date from the War Department," and that "they are entitled to full credence in the premises."

The instructions to the Peace Commissioners, referred to in the certificate, were dated Washington, April 12th, 1858, expressed the hope that they would reach their destination before hostilities were actually renewed, and instructing them to carry with them a proclamation of pardon for the treasonable acts of the Mormons, recently issued by the President, and give the same as extensive circulation as practicable. The Commissioners were not authorized to enter into any treaty or engagement with the Mormons, but to endeavor to induce them to return to their allegiance and render obedience to the laws and constitution. The Instructions included this clause of the President's proclamation to the people of Utah; "If you obey the law, keep the peace and respect the just rights of others, you will be perfectly secure, and may live in your present faith, or change it for another at your pleasure," and the Commissioners were instructed to impress this clause upon the Mormon mind, and to convince them if possible, that the government had never, directly nor indirectly, sought to molest them in their worship, to control them in their ecclesiastical affairs, or even to influence them in their religious opinions. They were also instructed to inform the Mormon leaders and people that it was the duty and determination of the federal government to see that the officials appointed and sent out by the President should be received and installed, and due obedience be yielded to the laws and their official acts.

Governor Powell and Major McCulloch left Washington at once for Great Salt Lake City, reporting to the Secretary of War from Fort Leavenworth April 25th, from Fort Kearney May 3rd, from Camp Scott, Utah (General Johnston's headquarters at Fort Bridger), June 1st, and from Great Salt Lake City, June 12th and 26th and July 3rd, and, on their return, from Washington City August 24th, 1858.

The Commissioners arrived in the city of the saints on the 7th of June, and on the 12th of that month they reported to the Secretary of War;

"We lost no time in placing ourselves in communication with the chief men of the Mormon people. After the fullest and freest conference with them we are pleased to state that we have settled the unfortunate difficulties existing between the government of the United States and the people of Utah. We are informed by the people and chief men of the territory that they will cheerfully yield obedience to the constitution and laws of the United States. They consent that the civil officers of the territory shall enter upon the discharge of their respective duties. They will make no resistance to the army of the United States in its march to the valley of Salt Lake or elsewhere. We have their assurance that no resistance will be made to the officers, civil or military, of the United States in the exercise of their various functions in the territory of Utah."

How changed the sentiments of Bombastes Furioso since the preceding autumn;

But Governor Cumming had, seventeen days previously, announced to General Johnston that peace had been declared. The Governor had gone into the city early in April (the 7th) and had everywhere been cordially received and hospitably entertained by the military, municipal, territorial and church authorities and by the people at large, and everywhere recognized as the Governor of Utah. Instead of Brigham Young placing him in his own carriage and sending him back (as he assured Captain Van Vliet he would do), Brigham called upon him, tendered him the territorial seal and other public property, and evinced a willingness to afford him every facility which he might require for the efficient performance of his administrative duties, and all this, in the opinion of Governor Cumming, with the approval of a majority of the community.

On his return to Camp Scott (General Johnston's headquarters at Fort Bridger), May 21st, 1858 eleven days before the commissioners got out there, seventeen days before they reached the city and twenty-two days before they reported to the Secretary of War that they had "settled the unfortunate difficulties" Governor Cumming wrote General Johnston as follows:

"After a careful investigation, I am gratified in being able to inform you that I believe there is at present no organized armed force of its inhabitants in any part of this territory, with the exception of a small party subject to my orders, in or near Echo Canyon."

Governor Cumming has been so informed by Brigham Young, in addition to passing all the points theretofore heavily garrisoned by Mormon militia, and upon receipt of this information General Johnston promptly declared the territory open to the mails, to commercial pursuits, and to the free intercourse of the inhabitants.

Therefore, it was not the Peace Commissioners, nor yet was it Governor Cumming, who took the bombast out of Brigham and struck terror to the souls of the saints it was the rapid approach of 3,912 reinforcements for Johnston's army, which would bring his fighting strength up to 6,500 men of all arms, with from 1,800 or 2,000 wagons heavily loaded with supplies, accompanying the reinforcements.

These reinforcements, which began to move out from Fort Leavenworth about the 1st of May, 1858, consisted of 890 officers and men of the First Cavalry, two companies (176 officers and men) of the Second Dragoons, two light companies (180 officers and men) of the Second Artillery, 878 officers and men of the Sixth Infantry, 878 officers and men of the Seventh Infantry, and sixteen staff officers. General W. S. Harney also started out with one of these columns, but was ordered back after reaching Cottonwood Springs. General Scott himself was to have sailed from New York February 5th for California, clothed with full powers for an effective diversion or co-operation in Johnston's favor from that quarter, and General Johnston was so informed officially from headquarters under date of January 23rd, 1858, but the general-in-chief afterward abandoned the project.

The capriciousness of Brigham Young, the wily autocrat of the Mormons, is well illustrated by a sermon called "instructions to

Israel," delivered by him in the tabernacle March 28th, 1858, and published in the Deseret News, the official organ of the church, and his abject surrender to Governor Cumming alone ten days later. In that sermon he still breathed defiance and fire; said if the "licentious and corrupt soldiery," attempted to enter the valley before they (the Mormons) were ready they would "send them to their long homes," and admonished his people to prepare to burn their homes, hew down their trees and lay waste their fields. "It is a consolation to me", he said, "that I have the privilege of laying in ashes and in the dirt the improvements I have made, rather than those who would cut my throat, solely for my faith, shall inhabit my buildings and enjoy my fields and fruits." Yet he never lighted a torch nor chopped a tree.

A communication from Brigham Young to Colonel Kane of Philadelphia, dated Great Salt Lake City, March 9th, 1858, Tuesday, 8 o'clock p.m. and sent out to Fort Bridger by Brigham's son, Joseph A., and George Stringham, bears strong internal evidence that Colonel Kane had been in the city even prior to that date, as it wound up with the expression; "Trusting that you are rapidly regaining your health, and that success may attend you". In this note Brigham stated that he had just learned, through the southern Indians, "that the troops were very destitute of provisions", and offered to drive out nearly two hundred head of beef cattle belonging to Mr. Gerrish (formerly a Gentile merchant in the city), whom he supposed to be at General Johnston's headquarters, and would also, if acceptable, "send out fifteen or twenty thousand pounds of flour to the army, to which they will be perfectly welcome, or pay for, just as they choose". Colonel Kane immediately communicated this offer to General Johnston, who replied to Colonel Kane March 15th, 1858 as follows;

"Sir; President Brigham Young is not correctly informed with regard to the state of the supply of provisions of this army. There has been no deficiency, nor is there any now. We have abundance to last until the government can renew the supply. Whatever might be the need of the army under my command for food, we would neither ask nor receive from President Young and his confederates any supplies while they continue to be enemies of the government."

General Johnston also requested that his reply be communicated to Brigham Young. Colonel Kane was somewhat shocked at the reply and appealed to General Johnston to modify it, saying; "I fear it must greatly prejudice the public interest to refuse Mr. Young's proposal in such a manner at the present time," but there the correspondence on that subject closed.

Nor withstanding this snub, about one month later, April 16th, 1858, Brigham Young made another attempt to conciliate the army before it could get at him, by addressing the following note to Governor Cumming who was then in the city;

"Sir; Learning that you propose sending an express to Colonel Johnson's camp, I avail myself of the opportunity of proffering, through your Excellency, to Colonel Johnston' and the army under his command, inasmuch as they are supposed to be measurably destitute, such supplies of provisions as we have, and they may need, prior to the arrival of supplies from the east.

"Trusting that you will appreciate the sincerity of the motives prompting this courtesy, I have the honor to be, very respectfully, your &c., Brigham Young".

As Governor Cumming went out to the army shortly after receiving this offer, he probably made it known to General Johnston orally, but the latter treated the matter with silent contempt.

On Sunday, April 8th, 1858, Brigham Young, with apparent reluctance revealed a great "secret" in his sermon in the Tabernacle, in the following characteristic style;

"I have a good mind to tell a secret right here; I believe I will tell it anyhow; they say there is a fine country down south there; Sonora is it, is that your name for it? Do not speak of this out of doors, if you please".

He had already ordered an exodus from the northern settlements, and from Great Salt Lake City itself, and the roads were every where filled with wagons loaded with provisions and household furniture, the women and children, often without shoes or hats, driving their flocks, they knew not where.[##] They seemed not only resigned but

[##] The peace commissions in their final report to the Secretary of War from Great Salt Lake City, July 3rd, 1858, said; "We were informed by various (discontented) Mormons who had lived in the settlements north of Provo

cheerful, according to the report of Governor Cumming to General Lewis Cass, Secretary of State. "It is the will of the Lord," they would say, and they seemed to rejoice to exchange the comforts of home for the trials of the wilderness. Their ultimate destination was not known to them. "Going south" seemed sufficiently definite for most of them, but many believed that their ultimate destination was Sonora. By the 2nd of May 1858, Brigham Young, Heber C. Kimball, and most of the influential men had left their commodious mansions in the city, without apparent regret, to lengthen the long train of wanderers. The masses everywhere announced to Governor Cumming that the torch would be applied to every house, indiscriminately, throughout the country, so soon as the troops should attempt to cross the mountains, and men were left behind avowedly for that purpose. The emigrants halted in Utah Lake Valley, about fifty miles south of the city, and most of them encamped in and about the town of Provo, whither Governor Cumming and later Peace Commissioners Powell and McCulloch, followed them and persuaded them to return to their homes.

Meantime, during the winter, and especially about the approach of spring, the Mormons began to get a taste of the medicine they had been so long preparing for the American army and people, in the way of Indian raids. The eastern Utes had committed slight depredations in the immediate vicinity of Great Salt Lake City, and the Mormons, doubtless thinking the Americans had adopted their own tactics, accused Agent Hurt, and incidentally General Johnston, of having

---

that they had been forced to leave their homes and go to the southern part of the territory; that they desired to remain at their residences, and would have done so had they not been threatened with forcible ejection. We were also informed that at least one-third of the persons who had removed from their homes were compelled to do so. We were told that many were dissatisfied with the Mormon Church, and would leave it whenever they could with safety to themselves. We are of opinion that the leaders of the church congregated the people in order to exercise more immediate control over them, and thus prevent their secession from the church. It is strikingly evident that the priesthood exercises very great control over the masses and their polity manifestly tends to centralization of wealth, and both ecclesiastical and temporal power in the church".

incited the Indians to these acts. This accusation was overwhelmingly refuted by affidavits and other statements of numerous officers and employees of the government, mountaineers,

Old Indian traders of the country, and by one prominent Mormon (B. F. Cummings) residing in the northern part of the Territory, and who had recaptured a portion of the stock stolen by the northern Indians.

Ben F. Ficklin, a mountaineer well acquainted all over the interior of the continent, had been dispatched by General Johnston, December 9th, 1857, to the Flathead Indian country on the headwaters of the Missouri and Columbia rivers to procure cattle and horses, and did not get back to Fort Bridger until April 10th, 1858. About the first of March of that year, while Ficklin was in the Flathead country, three hundred miles from the scene of disturbance and with two massive and rugged ranges of mountains and from two to six feet of snow between, a band of Bannock and Snake Indians attacked a fortified Mormon settlement at the confluence of Blackfoot creek and Snake river, on the old Fort Hall and Oregon trail, killed two Mormons and wounded three, killed and run off all of their cattle (about three hundred head) and most of their horses because the Mormons had furnished a party of Nez Perce' Indians arms and ammunition to make war on them (the Bannocks and Snakes). Ficklin, with his party of ten men, twelve horses and six mules, suffered intensely from cold, hunger and fatigue, and lost nine animals. During the thirty days occupied by his return trip he had twenty-six days of rain or snow. The worst of it was, however, that his mission proved a failure, as both the mountaineers and Indians of the North Country were afraid to drive cattle or horses to the army for fear they would be attacked or robbed on the way by the Mormons.

The only reference General Johnston made to the Mormon charges against himself, Indian Agent Hurt and Mr. Ficklin (contained in two letters to Governor Cumming from Wm. H. Hooper, Secretary pro tem. under Brigham Young, both dated April 15th, 1858) was in the closing paragraph of his report to army headquarters, under date of April 22nd, 1858, as follows;

"Copies of letters of the superintendent of Indian affairs, the agent, Dr. Hurt, and copies of affidavits herewith, not only contain a complete refutation of the charges, but show that persons among them (the Mormons), by their own improper conduct, have brought the hostilities they complain of upon themselves."

As before stated, Governor Cumming first arrived in Great Salt Lake City April 12, 1858. He had passed through armed parties of Mormons at Lost and Yellow creeks and in Echo canyon, and at every point he was recognized as the governor of Utah and tendered a military salute. It was arranged for the Governor to be taken through Echo canyon at night, as to keep him from seeing the fortifications bristling through that gorge for miles, but the canyon was brilliantly illuminated with bon fires from base to brow of the mountains on both sides, in honor of the representative of the executive authority of the United States in the territory.

On the 24th of April the governor was informed that a number of persons who were desirous of leaving the territory were unable to do so, and considered them-selves to be unlawfully restrained of their liberty. He caused public notice to be given immediately of his readiness to relieve all persons who were or deemed themselves to be aggrieved; and on the following day, which was Sunday, he requested the following notice to be read in his presence to the people in the Tabernacle;

"It has been reported to me that there are persons residing in this and in other parts of the territory who are illegally restrained of their liberty. It is therefore proper that I should announce that I assume the protection of all such persons, if any there be, and request that they will communicate to me their names and places of residence, under seal, through Mr. Fay Worthen, or to me in person during my stay in the city.

"A. Cumming, Governor of Utah."

Thereafter he kept his office open at all hours of the day and night, and during the first week registered no less than fifty-six men, thirty-three women and seventy-one children, as desirous of his protection and assistance in proceeding to the states. The large majority of these people were of English birth, and stated that they left the congregation from a desire to improve their circumstances, and to realize elsewhere more money by their labor. Certain leading men among the Mormons also promised Governor Cumming that they would furnish these apostates flour and assist them in leaving the country. Six months prior to that time, at least the fifty-six men would have been put to death had they attempted to apostatize.

In the Tabernacle on that same Sunday (April 25th, 1858), as Governor Cumming afterward wrote Secretary Cass, he had a "time" that would be remembered by him as "an occasion of intense interest". Brigham Young introduced him by name to an audience of between 3,000 and 4,000 as the governor of Utah, and in a discourse of half an hour's duration the governor touched boldly upon the leading questions at issue between them and the general government. The audience listened respectfully to all he had to say, and, as he fancied, approvingly when he explained to them what he intended should be the character of his administration. But after closing his remarks the governor again got up and stated that he would be glad to hear from any who might be inclined to address him upon topics of interest to the community. This threw down the bars, and, in the slang of the day, "the calves got out". The invitation brought forth in succession several fiery and powerful speakers, who evidently exercised great influence over the masses of the people. They harangued on the subject of the assassination of Joseph Smith and his friends; the services rendered by the Mormon battalion in the Mexican War "to an ungrateful country", their sufferings on the "plains" during their dreary pilgrimage to their mountain home, etc. The congregation became greatly excited, and joined the speakers in their intemperate remarks, finally exhibiting such frenzy that Governor Cumming became alarmed. At length, however, the efforts of Brigham Young were successful in calming the tumult and restoring order before the adjournment of the meeting.

May 12th, 1858, Governor Cumming wrote Secretary Cass to announce that the road was then open between Missouri and California, and that emigrants and others adopting the usual precautions for their safety against the Indians might pass through Utah territory without hindrance or molestation.

May 25th, 1858, Governor Cumming wrote General Johnston that Marshal F. K. Dotson had called upon him for such posse as would enable him to serve writs of arrest upon Brigham Young and sixty-six others indicted for treason and other felonies, by the grand jury in Green river county, Utah territory, and asking if the commander could furnish such a posse. On the following day General Johnston replied that he would not, at that time, be able to comply with such a requirement.

Governor Powell and Major McCulloch, the peace commissioners, arrived at Fort Bridger May 29th, 1858, and after a full consultation with General Johnston and Governor Cumming (who had come out from the city) left on the 2nd of June for Great Salt Lake City, where they arrived on the 7th. Brigham Young and other chief men of the Mormon church were then at Provo, fifty miles south, to which place and to points beyond, the inhabitants of the settlements north of the city and the larger portion of the people of the city also had gone with their families and personal property. On their arrival the commissioners at once made known the object of their mission, and on the evening of the 8th they were waited upon by a committee of three Mormons who informed them that it was the desire of the people of the territory that they (the commissioners) confer with ex-governor Brigham Young concerning the difficulties between the United States government and the people of Utah. The commissioners replied that they would with pleasure confer with ex-governor Young and such others as the people of Utah should indicate as their representatives, at such time and place as was convenient to them. The next evening the committee informed them that ex-governor Young and other chief men of the Mormon Church would be in the city on the evening of the 10th, and would confer with them at 9 o'clock on the morning of the 11th.

At the appointed hour the commissioners met, in the large room of the council house, ex-governor Brigham Young, Heber C. Kimball, Lieutenant General Daniel H. Wells (constituting the first presidency of the church of Latter Day Saints), several of the Twelve apostles and other chief men of the church, and stated very fully the object of their mission. Brigham Young, General Wells, Erastus Snow, Mr. Clements and Major Hunt made speeches in reply, all professing attachment to the constitution of the United States and gratification that the President had sent out the commissioners. After several hours the conference adjourned until 9 o'clock next day.

On the morning of the 12th the conferees again met at the same place, a large number of citizens being present, speeches being made by Elder John Taylor, Colonel George A. Smith, General Furgison and Brigham Young. The result of this conference was that the Mormon authorities and people agreed that the officers, civil and military, of the United States, should enter the territory without resistance, and exercise peaceably and unmolested all the functions of their various offices. All present appeared gratified at the result of the conference.

Subsequently the commissioners wrote out "a concise statement of what was said in the conference," and Brigham Young added thereto his certificate that it was "in substance a correct statement of what was said in said conference," and this document was submitted to the Secretary of War August 24th, 1858, after the return of the Commissioners to Washington.

June 8th, 1858, Major and Brevet Colonel Wm. Hoffman of the Sixth Infantry arrived at General Johnston's headquarters with a portion of his command and the first division of the supply train from Fort Laramie. On the 10th Captain Hendrickson arrived (through a snow storm) with the other portion of the escort and the remainder of the supply trains; and on the 11th the commands of Colonel Loring and Captain Marcy arrived from New Mexico. Being now supplied with reinforcements, subsistence; horses and mules, General Johnston determined to advance toward Great Salt Lake City on the 13th of June.

On the 12th of June the peace commissioners had written to General Johnston from the city informing him that the difficulties had been settled, that there would be no opposition to his entrance, and suggested that he march to the valley as soon as it was convenient for him to do so suggesting, at the same time, that he issue a proclamation to the people of Utah to allay their apprehension of trespass by the army upon their rights and property. Accordingly on the 14th of June

General Johnston issued and sent forward for circulation the following;

To the People of Utah.

The commissioners of the United States, deputed by the President to urge upon the people of this territory the necessity of obedience to the constitution and laws as enjoined by his proclamation, have this day informed me that there will be no obstruction to the administration and execution of the laws of the federal government, nor any opposition on the part of the people of this territory to the military force of the government in the execution of their orders. I therefore feel it incumbent on me, and have great satisfaction in doing so, to assure those citizens of the territory who, I learn, apprehend from the army ill treatment, that no person whatever will be in anywise interfered with or molested in his person or rights, or in the peaceful pursuit of his avocations; and, should protection be needed, that they will find the army (always faithful to the obligations of duty) as ready to assist and protect them as it was to oppose them while it was believed they were resisting the laws of their government.

A. S. Johnston,
Colonel 2nd Cavalry and Brevet
Brig. Gen., commanding

Meantime, however, Governor Cumming had become greatly alarmed on learning that General Johnston had determined to take up the line of march, even as early as the 15th of June as the Governor, at the conference between the Mormon leaders and the peace commissioners, had given a prompt and positive denial to the statement of Brigham Young that the latter had evidence of General Johnston's intention to advance the army on the 14th or 15th of June, without waiting for communications from the commissioners or the governor. Accordingly the Governor wrote, June 15th, very earnestly to the General to make some explanation that would relieve him (the governor) from seeming duplicity.

General Johnston replied from Yellow Creek, June 19th, that at his conference with the commissioners and the governor it being understood that he could not commence the march from Fort Bridger before the arrival of supplies, and that the preparation for the march, depending upon their arrival, could not probably be made before the 15th or 20th instant, and understanding from them that they believed before that time they would be able to ascertain the result of their mission he did say, as represented by the governor, that he would delay the march of the troops until he heard from them; but by no means did he intend to give to what he said the binding force of a pledge, should it be in confliction with a good military reason for pursuing a different course, nor did he suppose they would so understand it.

Notwithstanding the alarm of the Governor, General Johnston commenced his forward movement on the 13th of June 1858, the advance column from Fort Bridger reaching Bear River the next day, the second column on the 15th and the rear guard and remainder of the supply trains on the 16th. Finding that the army was advancing steadily though slowly, Governor Cumming seems to have become intensely alarmed, lest General Johnston should come into the city or go into camp near it, and thus "cause unnecessary irritation," in "the present excited condition of the public mind," and wrote General Johnston on the 17th of June that he deemed it his "duty to protest against your occupancy of positions in the immediate vicinity of this city or other dense settlement of the population," concluding with the solemn and awful warning; "Should you resolve to act in opposition to my solemn protest, you may be assured that it will result in disastrous consequences, such as cannot be approved by our government."

Disregarding both the solemn protest and awful warning of Governor Cumming, near midday on Saturday, June 26, 1858, General Johnston marched his whole army right through the heart of Great Salt Lake City, taking the main street between the tithing house and Temple, passing within half a block of Brigham's Lion and Beehive mansions, the regimental bands, by order, playing "Jordan am a hard road to travel," and marched out across the Jordan river and went into camp, where he remained several days, everybody in the city (except Governor Cummings perhaps) laughing at the air selected (as they supposed) by the bands in passing through the city.

Meantime, on the 14th of June, Governor Cumming had issued the following proclamation;

TO THE INHABITANTS OF UTAH AND OTHERS WHOM IT MAY CONCERN.

Whereas, James Buchanan, President of the United States, at the city of Washington, the sixth day of April, eighteen hundred and fifty-eight, did by his proclamation offer to the inhabitants of Utah who submit to the laws a free and full pardon for all treasons and seditions heretofore committed; and

Whereas, the proffered pardon was accepted, with the prescribed terms of the proclamation, by the citizens of Utah;

Now, therefore I, Alfred Cumming, governor of Utah territory, in the name of James Buchanan, President of the United States, do proclaim that all persons who submit themselves to the laws and to the authority of the federal government are by him freely and fully pardoned for all treasons and seditions heretofore committed. All criminal offenses associated with or growing out of the overt acts of sedition and treason are merged in them, and are embraced in the "free and full pardon" of the President. And I exhort all persons to persevere in a faithful submission to the laws and patriotic devotion to the constitution and government of our common country.

Peace is restored to our territory.

All civil officers, both federal and territorial, will resume the performance of the duties of their respective offices without delay, and be diligent and faithful in the execution of the laws. All citizens of the United States in this territory will aid and assist the officers in the performance of their duties.

Fellow citizens, I offer to you my congratulations for the peaceful and honorable adjustment of recent difficulties.

Those citizens who have left their homes I invite to return as soon as they can do so with propriety and convenience.

To all I announce my determination to enforce obedience to the laws, both federal and territorial.

Trespass upon property, whether real or personal, must be scrupulously avoided.

Gaming and other vices are punished by territorial statutes with peculiar severity and I commend the perusal of these statutes to those persons who may not have had an opportunity of doing so previously.[##]

In testimony where of I have here unto set my hand and caused the official seal of the territory to be affixed, at Great Salt Lake City, in the territory of Utah, this fourteenth day of June, one thousand eight hundred and fifty-eight, and of the independence of the United States the eighty-second.

A. Cumming.
By the Governor; John Hartnett, Secretary.

July 8th, 1858, General Johnston reported to army headquarters from the north end of Cedar Valley, thirty-six miles southwest from Great Salt Lake City, that he had established the camp of the army of Utah at that place (afterward known as Camp Floyd), and designed to make it permanent. Cedar Valley occupied a commanding position, debouching in the direction of Great Salt Lake City by two routes, also by two towards Provo and into Tintic valley, in the direction of Fillmore City and other southern settlements, and the force, if called for, could be promptly applied either in the direction of Great Salt Lake City or Provo, the two places being about equidistant from the camp, the former a little east of north and the latter southeast. Besides, Cedar Valley was an ideal place for a military post, being eight miles in width and twenty-five miles long, being connected with both Rush and Tintic valleys, and all three of them affording fine grazing. Cedar Valley lies parallel to Utah Lake (fresh water) and only three miles distance westerly, with a low range of mountains intervening. In the same communication General Johnston, anticipating the early arrival of General W. S. Harney or Colonel Edwin V. Sumner, wrote;

[##] Timely and kindly warning to the soldiers and other invading Gentiles, nearly all of whom were given to gambling.

"On the arrival of General Harney or Colonel Sumner, I desire to be ordered to join my regiment. If that cannot be granted, I request that the General will grant me a furlough for four months, with leave to apply for an extension. I have had no relaxation from duty, not for a day, for more than nine years."

July 19th, 1858, General Johnston ordered Colonel W. W. Loring of the Rifle Regiment to return to the department of New Mexico with his four companies of riflemen, recently employed in guarding the small party of Captain Marcy and his several hundred head of horses and mules from New Mexico to Utah, the command to follow what was known as the "southern route," via Lake Utah, Green River, up White river, etc. Larue, an intelligent guide with Colonel Loring, representing it as quite practicable as a wagon route, and several hundred miles shorter than the one by which the command had come. On the same date General Johnston ordered Lieutenant Colonel Barnard E. Bee to move with the three companies of volunteers (teamsters, herders, laborers and other attaches of contractors, and other trains who had enlisted the previous winter) for Fort Leavenworth, where they were to be paid off and discharged.

In July, 1858, the Utah Indians (now commonly called the Utes) began to practice Mormon tactics by stealing horses out about Fort Bridger, where Major and Brevet Lieutenant Colonel W. Hoffman of the Sixth Infantry was in command. About the 20th ten or more Utes visited a timber camp on Black's Fork, about ten miles above Bridger, behaved very impudently, and helped themselves to the men's rations. The next night ten horses were stolen from a Snake Indian on the Muddy, a few miles from Bridger, and on the night of the 26th four horses and two mules were stolen from the post. Two parties were dispatched in pursuit, one of four men under Lieutenant Bell following the foot of the mountain along Henry's Fork to its mouth. As he progressed, other trails came into the one he was following, showing a pretty strong party of mounted men. Toward sunset the second day he came suddenly upon seven or eight Indians, and he recognized in their possession two of the animals, which had been stolen. From the fact the Indians seemed to have no fear of him he was disposed to be a little cautious, and very soon some thirty Indians showed themselves, some on foot and some mounted. With such a force before him he had no alternative but to retire, which he did. At this there was a show of pursuit on the part of the Indians, more in bravado perhaps than with any serious intention of an attack. Some of the Indians fired off their guns, shouted, and made other signs of defiance. They made two or three threats of a charge, but on Lieutenant Bell's facing them they kept out of range. They followed him two or three miles and then disappeared. On the 30th Colonel Hoffman sent out a party of about forty mounted men to scour the region thoroughly, but the Indians had disappeared, nor did they attempt any depredations afterward.

August 16th, 1858, the camp of the four-mule mail coach from Utah to Placerville, Cal. with John Mayfield as driver and Daniel W. Thomas and Washington Perkins as passengers, was attacked by Shoshone and Bannock Indians near Thousand Springs valley on the Humboldt river, three hundred miles west of Great Salt Lake City, and all the mules run off. The three men remained in the camp a day and a half, waiting for the mail coach from the west, but the Indians gathered about them in such numbers and in such a threatening manner that they gathered up the mail, their blankets and some provisions and started back on foot to the Goose Creek station, about 100 miles. The Indians followed in great numbers, and the men finally dropped all of their loose effects, and during the temporary halt of the Indians to dispose of the plunder, the whites took to the mountains in the night, and finally reached the Goose Creek station on the evening of the 25th. As the same route was also lined with emigrants who were frequently attacked and robbed and murdered by the Indians, General Johnston promptly ordered Captain J. M. Hawes of the Second Dragoons to take one hundred dragoons and fifty infantry to the first crossing of the Humboldt river and to establish camp there on or in sight of the road until about the first of November, or until the season's travel was over; to ascertain to what band or tribe the robbers belonged and to demand of the chief the restoration of the mail and other property stolen, and in case of failure to comply with these demands, or on indication of hostility at any time, to punish them for past offenses to the full extent of his power. Howard Egan, well acquainted with the road and climate, and in addition an interpreter, accompanied Captain Hawes' command from Great Salt Lake City.

On the 10th of September 1858, two Indians, supposed to belong to Pinteet's band of Utes on the public reservation forty-five miles southeast of Camp Floyd, outraged a Mrs. Markham and her nine-year old daughter (Mormons) near Spanish Fork. Indian Agent Hurt went to the place and demanded the surrender of the Indians, which was refused. He then appealed to Governor Cumming, who applied to General Johnston for a posse comitatus to arrest the Indians, three in number, a third one having been present when the outrages were committed. General Johnson dispatched one hundred dragoons and one hundred infantry, under command of Major G. R. Paul, to the reservation. Major Paul arrived at the place at day-break on the morning of the 2nd of October, and immediately surrounded the Indian village. There were not more than a dozen men in the village, the others having left for the mountains on the morning of September 30th. Those present attempted to escape, but were pursued and nearly all captured, Chief Pintects himself being fired upon and killed. By detaining one chief and several of his band in custody and releasing the others, they promised to bring in the guilty young bucks which they did, and all were released except the culprits, who were taken to Great Salt Lake City for trial. The third was not to be found; but it was conceded by all that, though present, he had nothing to do with the outrages committed.

This transaction caused considerable alarm among the Mormon settlers about Spanish Fork, Springville and Pond Town, who feared an Indian uprising on account of it, and on learning this General Johnston ordered Major Paul to remain at Spanish Fork and ordered one hundred men each to Springville and Pond Town, provisioned until the 25th of October.

In September, 1858, General Johnston directed J. H. Simpson, Captain Corps Topographical Engineers, to explore and open a new route from Camp Floyd to Fort Bridger, and this work was completed by the 15th of October, the new road being about the same length (155 miles) as that through Weber and Echo canyons, and far superior in grades, grass, water and wood, and not so readily blocked by snow.

CHAPTER VIII

Indian Wars Incited By Mormons

Show conclusively that the Mormons had sent numerous emissaries among the northwestern Indians to stir them up to hostilities against the government. Even Brigham Young himself went up among the Flatheads and Nez Perces in the spring of 1857, and was represented to them as Choosuklee (Jesus Christ), ##(See pages 61-62) telling them that he would come again after-a-while, when the whites would be sent out of the country and all would be well for the Indians. The Mormon church authorities also sent Snake Indians under their control among the Nez Perces, Cayuse, and Walla-Walla tribes to tell them that the Mormons were anxious to supply them with arms, ammunition, cattle and everything that they might wish. Ira Hatch, a noted Mormon missionary among Indians, was sent down among the Navajoes, a powerful and wealthy tribe of northern Arizona and western New Mexico, in the summer of 1857, and was met at Las Vegas (then in southern Utah but now believed to be in Nevada) by the first party of Gentiles who passed over the Mountain Meadows after the massacre, a party that would doubtless have been massacred but for the timely arrival of this missionary, who had great influence over the Vegas and Muddy Indians, by 150 of whom this small party was surrounded. Hatch made no concealment of the fact that he had been on a mission to the Navajo country, and said he was then on his way to Great Salt Lake City to report the result to Brigham Young. Many Mormons doubted Ira Hatch's fealty to the church, and suspected he was pretending to be loyal to the faith until such time as he would be afforded an opportunity to "get even" for the assassination of his brother, whom Bill Hickman, one of the four captains of Danites or Destroying Angels, had shot in the back of the head while young Hatch was lying face down drinking from a spring of water. But Brother Ira appears to have been faithful to the last.

The machinations of these Mormon missionaries bore abundant fruit in 1858, to the irreparable loss of all, and almost extermination of some, of the Indian tribes who listened to them and depended upon the false promises of Brigham Young and his followers.

The first and oftenest approached Indians were the first to break out, in Washington territory. While Brevet Lieutenant Colonel E. J. Steptoe, with two howitzers, five company officers and 152 enlisted men of the First Dragoons and Ninth Infantry, was passing through the Spokane country, in Washington, en route from Walla-Walla to Colville, on Sunday morning, May 16th, 1858, and when near the To-hoto-nim-me, he found himself suddenly in the presence of 1,200 Indians of various tribes Spokanes, Pelouses, Coeurd' Alenes, Yakimas, and some others all armed, painted and defiant. He moved slowly on until just about to enter a ravine that wound along the bases of several hills, which were all crowned with the excited savages. Perceiving that it was their purpose to attack him in this dangerous place, Colonel Steptoe turned aside and encamped, the whole wild frenzied mass moving parallel to the little column, and, by yells, taunts and menaces, apparently trying to drive them to some initiatory act of violence. Towards night a number of chiefs rode up to talk with the commander, and inquired what his motives were for this intrusion upon them. The commander replied that they were passing on to Colville, and had no hostile intentions toward the Spokanes, who had always been their friends, nor toward any other tribes who were friendly; that his chief aim in coming so far was to see the Indians and the white people at Colville (where there had already been some trouble because of isolated murders by the Indians), and, by friendly discussion with both, endeavor to strengthen their good feelings for each other. They expressed themselves satisfied, but would not consent to let him have canoes, without which it would be impossible for him to cross the Spokane river. For this reason Colonel Steptoe concluded to retrace his steps at once and the next morning, May 17th, turned back toward Fort Walla-Walla.

The command had not marched three miles when the Indians, who had gathered on the hills adjoining the line of march, began an attack upon the rear guard, and immediately the fight became general. The command labored under the great disadvantage of having to defend the pack train while in motion and in a rolling country peculiarly favorable to the Indian mode of warfare. They had only a small quantity of ammunition, but in their excitement, the soldiers could not be restrained from firing it in the wildest manner. The difficult and dangerous duty of flanking the great mass of Indians was assigned to Brevet Captain O. H. P. Taylor and Second Lieutenant William Gaston, both of the First Dragoons, and while the charge was successful in causing the enemy to fall back, both of these intrepid officers lost their lives. The Indians soon afterward returned the charge upon this company, which, having lost its officers, fell back in confusion and could not again be rallied.

About 1 p.m. after the loss of these officers and the demoralization of their company, Colonel Steptoe took possession of a convenient height and halted. Here the fight continued with unabated activity until night set in, the Indians occupying neighboring heights and working themselves along to pick off the soldiers. The wounded increased in number continually. Twice the enemy gave unmistakable evidence of a design to carry Colonel Steptoe's position by assault, and their number and desperate courage caused him to fear the most serious consequences from such an attempt. The following extract from Colonel Steptoe's official report of the affair is a graphic description of the result;

"It was manifest that the loss of their officers and comrades began to tell upon the spirit of the soldiers; that they were becoming discouraged, and not to be relied upon with confidence. Some of them were recruits but recently joined; two of the companies had musketoons which were utterly worthless in our present condition; and, what was most alarming, only two or three rounds of cartridges remained to some of the men and but few to any of them. It was plain that the enemy would give the troops no rest during the night, and they would be still further disqualified for stout resistance tomorrow, while the number of enemies would certainly be increased. I determined, for these reasons, to make a forced march to Snake river, about eighty-five miles distant, and secure the canoes in advance of the Indians, who had already threatened to do the same in regard to us. After consulting with the officers, all of whom urged me to the step as the only means, in their opinion, of securing the safety of the command, I concluded to abandon everything that might impede our march. Accordingly, we set out about 10 o'clock, in perfectly good order, leaving the disabled animals and such as were not in condition to travel so far and so fast, and with deep pain I have to add, the two howitzers. The necessity for this last measure will give you, as well as many words, a conception of the strait to which we believed ourselves to be reduced."

When General Scott received this report in the following July he endorsed to the Secretary of War thus;

> "This is a candid report of a disastrous affair. The small supply of ammunition is surprising and unaccounted for."

The Rev. Father P. Joset, S. J., of Vancouver was in the Spokane country at the time, and on hearing of the excited condition of the hostiles was hurrying to them to prevent an attack at the time it occurred, in a letter to the Rev. Father Congiato, said;

> "It appeared impossible that the troops could escape. In a position so critical, the Colonel deceived the vigilance of his enemies, and throwing them his provisions, as an inducement to delay, he defeated their plans; so if the troops have escaped, they owe it to the sagacity of the Colonel."

All the survivors who left the battle-ground at 10 o'clock on the night of the battle, May 18th, 1858, did escape, and not a shot was fired at them on their retreat.

This unpardonable assault upon and disastrous defeat of a small command aroused the military authorities on the Pacific coast to the highest pitch, although in Great Salt Lake City it caused genuine but somewhat subdued rejoicing.

Having concentrated all the available troops on the Pacific coast in Washington territory, and having moved his headquarters from San Francisco to Fort Vancouver, W. T., General N. S. Clarke, commander of that department, July 4th, 1858, ordered Colonel George Wright of the Ninth Infantry, then at Fort Dalles, Oregon territory (Oregon was admitted into the Union as a state February 12th,

1859) to proceed at once to Fort Walla-Walla and fit out a column of not less than 600 men and move as early as practicable after the first day of August against the Indians north and east of Fort Walla-Walla, the object to be attained being the punishment and submission of the Indians in the late attack on the command of Lieutenant Colonel Steptoe, and the surrender of the Pelouse Indians who had murdered two miners the previous April. Enclosed with the order was a copy of the terms of a treaty the general desired made with the friendly Nez Perces, as well as with the Coeur d'Alenes and the Spokanes, after their submission, with the further admonition that "whether such treaty be or be not made, hostages must be taken for their future good conduct." Colonel Wright was also instructed to make known to the Coeur d'Alenes and Spokanes the terms on which they could obtain peace; if they met him and accepted the terms well, if not he must make on them, as on the hostile Nez Perces and Pelouses, vigorous war. He was instructed to attack all the hostile Indians he might meet, with vigor, and to make their punishment severe and persevere until the submission of all was complete. The Coeur d'Alenes were to be given to understand that in peace or war their country must be open to the army. Colonel Wright had expressed his intention to declare martial law north of Snake River, but this was forbidden by General Clarke.

July 18th, 1858, General Clarke sent somewhat similar orders to Major Robert S. Garnett, of the Ninth Infantry, who was then commanding Fort Simcoe, W. T., who was to go against the hostiles in the Yakima country, and punish the Indians who had attacked a party of miners in the preceding June. He was to demand the delivery of the individual offenders, and if this was refused he was to drive the whole to submission by severe punishment. Hostages must also be demanded to insure the good behavior of the others. Chief Kamiakin and his son Qualchew could not longer be permitted to remain at large in the country; they must be surrendered or driven away, and no accommodation must be made with any who should harbor them; "let all know that an asylum given to either of these troublesome Indians, will be considered in future as evidence of a hostile intention on the part of the tribe."

The first "business" returns from these expeditions came from Major Garnett, who reported from camp on the upper Yakima river, August 15th, 1858, that at 3 o'clock that morning Second Lieutenant Jesse K. Allen of the Ninth Infantry, with fifteen mounted man, had surprised a hostile camp and captured twenty-one men, fifty women and children, seventy head of horses and fifteen head of cattle, besides considerable Indian property. In the affair unfortunately, Lieutenant Allen was accidentally shot and mortally wounded by one of his own men. Three of the bucks captured were recognized as among those who had attacked the miners, and were promptly shot.

Writing from camp on the Wenatcha river, August 30th, 1858, Major Garnett reported that on the 24th sixty men, under Lieutenant Crook of the Fourth Infantry, captured five more of the murderers of the two miners, and these were also shot by Major Garnett's orders. These, with one killed by Lieutenant Allen's party in the night attack and one shot by soldiers near Major Garnett's camp, made ten of the twenty-five who attacked the miners as having been made "good Indians." The summary treatment of these men very badly scared all of the Indians in that region, and perceptibly produced a salutary effect upon them. Six more of the twenty-five murderers were believed to be then in the mountains west of the Wenatcha, and the balance of them with Owhi, Qualchew, "Moses" and Skloom.

Colonel Wright, commanding the other column, did not see any Indians until August 29th, the day before he reached Four Lakes, 121 miles from Walla-Walla. On the morning of that day he saw a few of the enemy on distant hills, their numbers increasing during the day all moving parallel with his line of march. When he went into camp, late in the afternoon, the Indians approached his pickets and sharp firing commenced. Colonel Wright took out a portion of his command, but the Indians fled, and he made a fruitless pursuit for four miles. The enemy did not disturb the camp that night, but on the next day's march their numbers having greatly increased, they made a demonstration on the supply train, but were handsomely dispersed.

Early on the morning of September 1st, 1858, Colonel Wright, seeing large numbers of Spokane, Coeur e'Alene and Pelouse Indians collecting on the summit of a high hill two miles from his camp at Four Lakes, at 9 a.m. he marched against them with two squadrons of the First Dragoons under Brevet Major W. N. Grier, four companies of the Third Artillery (armed with rifle muskets) under Captain E. D. Keyes, a rifle battalion of two companies of the Ninth Infantry under Captain F. T. Dent, one mountain howitzer under Lieutenant J. L. White of the Third Artillery, and thirty friendly Nez Perce Indian allies under Lieutenant John Mullan of the Second Artillery. The camp was also left with a strong garrison of infantry and artillery under Captain J. A. Hardie. Major Grier was ordered to advance to the north and east around the base of the hill, while Colonel Wright advanced to the right with the remainder of the command, and when within six hundred yards of the Indians he ordered Captain Keyes to advance a company of his battalion, deployed, and drive the Indians from the hill. This was gallantly done, and the Indians were driven to the foot of the hill, and there rallied under cover of ravines, trees and bushes, keeping up a constant fire upon the two squadrons of dragoons, who were awaiting the arrival of the foot troops.

On reaching the crest of the hill Colonel Wright saw at once that the Indians were determined to measure their strength with him, showing no disposition to avoid a combat. In front lay a vast plain, with some four or five hundred mounted warriors, rushing to and fro, wild with excitement, and apparently eager for the fray; to the right, at the foot of the hill, in the pine forest, the Indians were also seen in large numbers.

Captain Keyes, with two companies of his battalion, was ordered to deploy along the crest of the hill, in rear of the dragoons, and facing the plains. The rifle battalion under Captain Dent, composed of two companies of the Ninth Infantry, was ordered to move to the right, and deploy in front of the pine forest, and the howitzer under Lieutenant White was advanced to a lower plateau, in order to gain a position where it could be fired with effect.

In five minutes the several battalions were in position, and Colonel Wright ordered an advance. Captain Keyes moved steadily down the long slope, passed the dragoons, and opened a sharp, well directed fire, which drove the Indians to the plains and pine forest; at the same time Captain Dent's rifle battalion, Lieutenant White's howitzer and Lieutenant Tyler's artillery company were hotly engaged with the Indians in the pine forest, the enemy constantly increasing in numbers by fugitives from the left.

Captain Keyes continued to advance, the Indians retiring slowly; Major Grier, with both squadrons, quietly leading his horses in the rear. At the signal the dragoons mounted, rushed with lighting speed through the intervals of skirmishes, charged the Indians on the plains overwhelmed them entirely, killed many, defeated and dispersed them all, and in a few minutes not a hostile Indian was to be seen on the plains. While this scene was being enacted, Dent, Winder and Fleming, with the rifle battalion, and Tyler and White, with the artillery company and howitzer, had pushed rapidly forward and driven the Indians out of the forest beyond view.

After a pursuit of more than a mile, both by dragoons and infantry until the last hostile disappeared from view, the troops were faced about and returned to camp at 2 p.m., having killed eighteen or twenty and wounded many hostiles, and without the loss of a soldier, either killed or wounded. All the officers and men engaged in the battle displayed the utmost coolness, courage and energy throughout the affair and none more so than the thirty Nez Perces.

Marching from Four Lakes to a point one mile and a half below the falls on Spokane river, W. T., September 6th, 1858, Colonel Wright again encountered, on the Spokane plains, a force of hostile Spokanes, Coeur e'Alenes, Pelouses and Pen d'Oreilles, numbering from five to seven hundred warriors, and fought, not only the Indians but prairie fires, for seven hours on a march of fourteen miles. The Indians attacked the troops and long pack trains in front and rear and on both flanks, and fired the grass wherever practicable. The column marched that day twenty-five miles without water, fighting fire and Indians continuously for seven hours, over a distance of fourteen miles, dragoons, infantry and artillery having frequently to charge through roaring flames to get at and rout the Indians; yet, while they killed two chiefs and two brothers of Chief Garey, and several of lesser note and wounded many others, the army had but one man slightly wounded and did not lose an animal. On the body of one of the chiefs killed was found a fine pistol worn by the lamented Second Lieutenant William Gaston of the First Dragoons, who fell in the affair with Lieutenant Colonel Steptoe at To-hoto-nim-me on the 16th of the preceding May.

On the morning of September 7th, 1858, Colonel Wright moved his column up the left bank of the Spokane to the ford, two miles above the falls. On the way up Indians appeared on the opposite bank and said that Chief Garey was near by and wanted to talk with the white chief. Colonel Wright told them to meet him at the ford, and soon after he went into camp at that point Garey crossed over. He said that he had always been opposed to fighting, but that the young men and many of the chiefs were against him, and he could not control them. Colonel Wright then told him to go back and say to all Indians and chiefs, for him;

"I have met you in two bloody battles; you have been badly whipped; you have lost several chiefs and many warriors killed and wounded. I have not lost a man or animal. I have a large force, and you Spokanes, Coeur D'Alenes, Pelouses, and Pen d'Oreilles may unite, and I can defeat you as badly as before. I did not come into this country to ask you to make peace; I came here to fight. Now, when you are tired of the war, and ask for peace, I will tell you what you must do; you must come to me with your arms, with your women and children, and everything you have, and lay them at my feet; you must put your faith in me and trust to my mercy. If you do this, I shall then dictate the terms upon which I will grant you peace. If you do not do this, war will be made on you this year and next, and until your nation shall be exterminated."

After this interview with Garey, the Chief Polotkin or Saulotken, with nine warriors, approached and desired an interview with Colonel Wright. They had left their rifles on the opposite side of the river, and Colonel Wright ordered the chief and seven of his warriors to sit while the other two were sent over to bring in the rifles. Saulotken was one of the three chiefs who had written to General Clarke through Rev. N. Congiato, S.L., of the Couer d'Alene Mission, that, "on account of the gold, maybe there will be no end of hostility," and that he would never give up any of his people to be executed or imprisoned for the murder of miners, nor would he ever give up his land. He had also been conspicuous in the assault upon and defeat of Colonel Steptoe on the 16th of May, and had been the leader in the battles with Colonel Wright on the 1st and 6th of the current month; so the commander detained the chief and one of his warriors who was strongly suspected of having been engaged in the murder of the two miners, and requested the chief to send out his other men to bring in the remainder of the band, with their arms and families.

Marching up the river again on the morning of September 8th, 1858, at a distance of nine miles a great cloud of dust was discovered in the mountains to the front and right, when Colonel Wright closed up his train, put it under a heavy guard, and ordered Major Grier to push rapidly forward with three companies of dragoons, while the commander himself followed with the foot troops. The Indians were driving off their stock, and had gone so far into the mountains that the dragoons had to dismount, but, after a sharp skirmish, succeeded in capturing at least eight hundred head of horses, the entire worldly wealth of the Palouse chief Til-co-ax. The further transactions of the day (September 8th) are thus laconically related by Colonel Wright in his official report to department headquarters:

"After camping that evening I investigated the case of the Indian prisoner suspected of having been engaged in the murder of the two miners; the fact of his guilt was established beyond doubt, and he was hanged at sunset."

On the 9th of September Colonel Wright sent two companies of foot and one troop of horse three miles above his camp, which was sixteen miles above Spokane Falls, to capture a herd of cattle, but they were so wild they could not be driven in. As he could not carry along the whole 800 head of horses, many of them wild as antelope, Colonel Wright replenished his own outfit from the herd and shot the remainder.

From the upper Spokane Colonel Wright marched to the Coeur d'Alene Mission, where he arrived on the 13th of September, where he found the Couer d'Alene Indians assembled in much alarm as to their fate, and ready to make peace on any terms that might be demanded of them. They had brought in and surrendered all the horses, mules, etc., they had stolen or captured, and readily signed the treaty of peace. The Pelouses, with their chiefs Kamiakin and Til-co-ax, were near by, and greatly frightened, but did not come in. In his official report from the mission Colonel Wright paid a high tribute to Rev.

Father J. Joset, S.J., "for his zealous and unwearied exertions in bringing all of these hostile Indians to an understanding of their true position," and added:

"The chastisement which these Indians have received has been severe but well merited and absolutely necessary to impress them with our power. For the last eighty miles our route has been marked by slaughter and devastation; 900 horses and a large number of cattle have been killed or appropriated to our own use; many barns with large quantities of wheat and oats, also many caches of vegetables, kamas, and dried berries, have been destroyed. A blow has been struck which they will never forget."

Colonel Wright, with his command, prisoners, hostages, and many other Coeur D'Alenes as guides, etc., left the mission on the 18th of September, for the vicinity of Colonel Steptoe's battle-ground, and went into camp on the Ned-whauld river, twelve miles north of the scene of that disaster, on the evening of the 22nd, with the expectation of meeting the Spokanes and Pelouses. Before reaching there he was advised that the whole Spokane nation were at hand, with their chiefs, headmen and warriors, ready and willing to submit to such terms, as he should dictate. Colonel Wright made the same demands upon them that he had made upon the Coeur d'Alenes. Speeches were made by the principal chiefs, who acknowledged their crimes, who expressed great sorrow for what they had done, and thankfulness for the mercy extended them. They stated that they were all ready to sign the treaty and comply with good faith with all its stipulations.

In the same camp, on the evening of September 23rd, the Yakima Chief Ow-hi presented himself before Colonel Wright. He came from the lower Spokane River, and told the colonel that he had left his son Qualchew at that place. Colonel Wright knew Ow-hi, had had dealings with him in the Yakima campaign in 1856, and knew that he was full of deceit and had been semi-hostile all the time. But he was exceedingly anxious to get hold of his son, Qualchew, one of the worst Indians in the country who had been actively engaged in all the murders, robberies and attacks upon the whites since 1855, both east and west of the Cascade mountains, and was known to have been one of the party who attacked some miners on the Wenatcha river the preceding June. So Colonel Wright seized Ow-hi and put him in irons, and then dispatched a messenger for Qualchew, desiring his presence forthwith, with notice that if he did not come he (Colonel Wright) would hang Ow-hi. The dutiful son ran all night in an effort to save the life of his father, and Colonel Wright told the result in his laconic manner in his official report of the 24th; "Qualchew came to me at 9 o'clock this morning, and at 9:15 a.m. he was hanged." Brevet Major Grier, with three troops of dragoons, returned to camp from the Steptoe battle-ground on the 25th of September with the bodies of Brevet Captain O.H.P. Taylor and Second Lieutenant William Gaston, and the two howitzers abandoned.

On the 26th of September Colonel Wright broke camp on the Ned-whauld (Lahtoo) river and started for the Pelouse River. On the evening before marching many of the Pelouse Indians began to gather around his camp. They represented themselves as having been in both battles, and when Kamiakin fled over the mountains they seceded from his party and were now anxious for peace. Colonel Wright seized fifteen men and after a careful investigation of their cases he found that they had left their own country and waged war against the forces of the United States, and one of them killed a sergeant of Colonel Steptoe's command, who was crossing the Snake river. He had promised those Indians severe treatment if found with the hostiles, and accordingly six of the most notorious were hanged on the spot. The others were ironed for the march.

September 30th, 1858, while Colonel Wright and his command were encamped on the Pelouse River, most of the Pelouse tribe came in to beg for peace. Colonel Wright then demanded the murderers of the two miners. One buck was brought out and hanged forthwith. One of these murderers had been hanged on the Spokane. Two of the men who stole cattle from Walla-Walla valley had been hanged at the Ned-whauld camp and one other killed in the battle at Four Lakes. All the property the Pelouses had belonging to the government was restored. Then Colonel Wright brought out his prisoners, and, finding that three of them were either Walla-Walla or Yakimas, they were hanged on the spot. Then the commander demanded of the tribe one chief and four men, with their families, to take to Fort Walla-Walla as hostages for the future good behavior of the others. This demand had been made of each tribe with which he had made peace, and in this and every other case complied with. He told the Pelouses he would not then make any written treaty of peace with them, but if they performed all he required that the next spring a treaty would be made with them. He told them that white people should travel through their country unmolested; that they should apprehend and deliver up every man of their nation who had been guilty of murder or robbery, all of which they promised him when he warned them that if he ever had to come into their country again on a hostile expedition no man should be spared, that he would annihilate the whole nation.

In his final official report to headquarters on his operations during the campaign, dated at Pelouse river camp, September 30th, 1858, announcing the close of the war, Colonel Wright wrote, under the sub-heading "results;"

1. Two battles fought by the troops under my command, against the combined forces of the Spokanes, Coeur d'Alenes, and Pelouses, in both of which the Indians were signally defeated, with a severe loss of chief and and warriors, either killed or wounded.
2. The Capture of one thousand horses, and a large number of cattle from the hostile Indians, all of which were either killed or appropriated to the service of the United States.
3. Many barns filled with wheat or oats, also several fields of grain, with numerous caches of vegetables, dried berries, and kamas, all destroyed, or used by the troops.
4. The Yakima Chief Ow-hi in irons, and the notorious war chief Qualchew hanged. The murderers of the miners, the cattle stealers et als. (in all eleven Indians), all hanged.
5. The Spokanes, Coeur d'Alenes and Pelouses entirely subdued, and sue most abjectly for peace on any terms.
6. Treaties made with the above named nations; they having restored all property, which was in their possession, belonging either to the United States or to individuals; they have promised that all white people shall travel through their country unmolested, and that no hostile Indians shall be allowed to pass through or remain among them.

7. The delivery to the officer in command of the United States troops of the Indians who commenced the battle with Lieutenant Colonel Steptoe contrary to the orders of their chiefs.
8. The delivery to the officer in command of the United States troops of one chief and four men, with their families, from each of the above named tribes, to be taken to Fort Walla-Walla, and held as hostages for the future good conduct of their respective nations.
9. The recovery of the two mounted howitzers abandoned by the troops under Lieutenant Colonel Steptoe.

CHAPTER IX

The Navajo War

So much for the maturely-considered machinations of the emissaries of the Mormon Church among the ignorant Indians of the northwest. Now for the fruits of "Brother" Ira Hatch's mission to the wealthy and powerful Navajo tribe in the south.

July 15th, 1858, W. T. H. Brooks, Captain in the Third Infantry and Brevet Major commanding Fort Defiance, New Mexico, in an official report to department headquarters at Santa Fe, stated that on the night of the 7th Indians had fired eight arrows into a hay camp he had established in the canyon a short distance from the post, one of the arrows killing a dog and three of them entering the tent wherein the hay-makers were sleeping; that on Monday, the 13th, a Navajo rode into the post, dismounted and hung around for three or four hours, trying to sell a couple of blankets, but acting suspiciously. Having sold a blanket to a camp woman, and within thirty yards of the door of Major Brook's quarters, he saw the latter's negro servant boy, Jim (a slave) coming towards him and pass to the rear of the camp woman's quarters; as Jim was about to pass him the Indian jumped upon his horse, and as soon as Jim's back was turned he fired an arrow, which passed under the boy's shoulder-blade into the lungs. The Indian immediately put whip to his horse and dashed over the hills. The boy made no exclamation, but at once pulled the arrow out of his back, but in doing so broke off the point in his lung, and died from the effects of the wound three days afterwards. The boy said he did nothing to the Indian, and was satisfied he had never seen him before.

The next day after the shooting Major Brooks sent for the head chief, Sarcillo Largo, and demanded that the assassin be given up, threatening war on the tribe if this was not complied with. The chief evaded any positive answer, and Major Brooks told him that if the murderer was not given up within twenty days he would make war on the tribe.

On the 22nd Major Brooks learned from what he deemed a reliable source, that the assassin of the negro boy belonged to an influential family of Kay-a-tana's band, then in the Yunecha mountains, and his people declared they would die before they would surrender him; that on the night before the shooting the assassin had a row with his wife wanted her to go some place with him, which she refused to do whereupon he tore every strip of clothing from her body at a dance, and, to appease his wrath, mounted his horse and rode away to kill some one outside of the tribe, as was the tribal custom.

Meantime owing to hostile demonstrations previously exhibited, one company under Lieutenant Averill had arrived to reinforce the garrison at Fort Defiance, and others were on the way.

Lieutenant Colonel D. S. Miles of the Third Infantry was appointed to the command of the Navajo expedition, and arrived at Fort Defiance on the 2nd of September with one company of Mounted Rifles and one company of the Fifth Infantry, aggregating 124 rank and file.

August 29th, at Bear Springs, en route to Fort Defiance, Captain McLane of the Mounted Rifles, with twelve men of his own company and fifty Mexican spies and guides under Captain Blas Lucero, was attacked by a large number of Navajoes, and after a short but sharp engagement, in which Captain McLane was wounded, six or eight Navajoes killed and many wounded and one Indian, twenty-five ponies and many blankets captured, the Indians retired.

September 8th, being the last day of grace for the Navajoes unless they delivered up the assassin of the negro boy, head chief Sarcillo Largo came into the post a day ahead and told Colonel Miles that he had become convinced the whites were in earnest, and that he would then say, what he never had before, that the murderer should be brought in, adding solemnly, that the chiefs and headmen were after him in every direction. Another wily savage named Sandoval displayed much concern at the near prospect of war, and for two or three days he had been running into the post and saying that the murderer had been seen near Bear Spring, then in a cave near Laguna Negrita, and another time at some other place. On the morning of the last day of grace Sandoval, with much parade, rushed through the garrison, stating, in his great haste, that the murderer was caught near

Chusca the previous afternoon. In a little white Sarcillo Largo and a few others came in to say that the murderer, when captured, was desperately wounded, and had died during the night, requesting a wagon to bring the body in. Colonel Miles ordered a pack mule instead, and after some delay, with great display on the part of the Indians, they brought in the dead body of a poor Mexican captive who had been a slave to one of the chiefs, and who had been murdered to save the real murderer and his coparceners in crime from the consequences of their heinous acts. These facts were fully brought out from Navajo captives during the war, which followed. Every individual witness, nearly every one of whom was familiar with the face of the real assassin, the moment he saw the body brought in, unhesitatingly pronounced it an imposture. Besides, this poor murdered Mexican captive had frequently visited the post, and was known to many of the older garrison. Sarcillo Largo and many other chiefs were waiting outside for a conference with Colonel Miles, but that officer sent word to them by Major Brooks that their falsehood had been exposed, that their attempted deception made them unworthy of further conference, and that therefore he would have nothing more to say to them.

On the 9th of September Colonel Miles marched from Fort Defiance with 309 men rank and file to open hostilities with the Navajoes. As various times prior to this date both Major Brooks and Colonel Miles, convinced from the bearing and behavior of the Navahoes that war was inevitable, had appealed to the commander of the department of New Mexico, General John Garland, to procure the co-operation of the Utah tribe, whom the Navajoes dreaded. This General Garland declined to attempt, as he had written General Johnston at Fort Bridger as early as the 24th of January proceeding that the Utahs were becoming impudent, and that a rumor, which he was inclined to believe, had reached him that these Indians were being tampered with by the Mormons. General Garland had also reported to army headquarters, January 31st, 1858, that an Indian had arrived from the Utah country, on a mission from the Utah Indians, charged with bringing about peace between the Navajoes and Utahs. This man had said he was sent by the Indians who were only ten days from Great Salt Lake City, and the Mormons were instigating these different tribes to bury their animosities, with a view, doubtless, in case of necessity, of arraying themselves against the United States government. This Indian emissary brought with him a certificate of baptism and membership in the church of Latter Day Saints.

Not with out standing these facts, and the fact that General Garland had reported that the Navajoes alone were "understood to number 2,500 warriors," Colonel Miles marched against them on the 9th of September with 309 men and nine officers. The Indians had frequently, with bravado, said they had collected at Canon de Chelly, where they intended to fight, and this determined Colonel Miles to march direct on that point and indulge them to their full contentment. On the second day's march the Mexican guides and spies in front brought in a well dressed fully armed, and well mounted Navajo, who was evidently spying out the army line of march. On questioning him, he said he was from Canon de Chelly, where there were a great number of Indians who intended to fight the soldiers. As this Indian seemed, from his appearance, of too much importance to release, and it would embarrass the column too much to retain him, Colonel Miles ordered him shot as a spy. In the afternoon of this date the Indians made their first appearance, on fleet horses, and were fired on, but at too long range for any damage.

On the third day out (September 11th) Colonel Miles' Zuni Indian guide conducted the column by a route evidently wholly unlooked for by the enemy, into the Canon de Chelly a frightful gorge, seventeen miles long, 1,200 to 1,500 feet deep, and having an average width of about 250 yards. Second Lieutenant Averill, of company F, Mounted Rifles, commanding the rear guard, had been fired upon, had one mule wounded in the knee, and had killed one Indian. Reaching water, Colonel Miles halted for the rear to close up, and detached Captain Elliott in command of his own and Captain Hatch's companies of the Mounted Rifles, to sweep through the canyon to its mouth if possible, and rejoin the column, if he thought it could not reach there before dark. Soon after he left Captain Elliott sent back a squaw and child captured. Colonel Miles marched with the infantry. The heights around were covered with Indians, occasionally firing on the troops. In a mile or so more an Indian was discovered to the left; chase was given by two or three Mexicans, three mounted orderlies and Assistant Surgeon McKee. The buck escaped, but they captured a squaw and two children. Directly after this Colonel Miles saw an Indian creeping through a corn-field to the right, and himself and Lieutenant Hildt gave chase and soon overtook and captured him. He proved to be an old man, and Colonel Miles did not kill him, but found him to be useful afterward. Soon afterward Captain Elliott was met, returning, having failed to reach the mouth of the canyon, through lack of daylight. He had had a fight with ten Indians, killed one certain and probably more and wounded several. A wide place was selected in the canyon and the troops went into camp. The moment they stopped the Indians opened fire on them from the north wall. Colonel Miles asked his captive if he knew who commanded the Indians on the north side, to which he replied that his son was there. The commander then told him to call to the Indians that if they shot an arrow or fired a gun into camp that night he (Miles) would surely hang him (the captive) next morning. The old fellow called lustily and prayed to them to cease firing, which they did immediately, and the camp was not molested during the night.

Early on the morning of the 12th the column moved down the canyon. Captain Elliott had informed the colonel that at a narrow place below he had been fired upon from the walls, and where the Indians had rolled down huge blocks of stone, which crumbled to dust before reaching the bottom. Colonel Miles sought and soon found a place on the south side where he could throw up the infantry companies, who soon cleared the edges of the canyon on both sides, and the command passed through in safety, to the mouth of the great gorge and encamped in an extensive corn field, where the men feasted on green corn and peaches.

While thus enjoying themselves, Indians in great numbers hovered around, giving the soldiers, in the afternoon, the opportunity of practicing at long range with their rifles, and no doubt several of the enemy were wounded, and one was seen to reel and fall from his horse.

A chief of great importance among the Navajoes, named Nak-risk-thlaw-nee, showed a white flag. Colonel Miles sent his adjutant, Lieutenant Walker of the Third Infantry, out to see what was wanted. The chief commenced by saying that the murderer was not there; that he wanted peace, and what were they there for, eating up his corn? The adjutant delivered the commander's reply, *"That"* he (the Chief) could have peace if he delivered up the murderer, and that he had no talk for anyone until that was done.

The useful old captive informed Colonel Miles that about twelve miles south, over some high, red hills, which could be seen from camp, were several lakes, where there were large herds and many Indians. Captain Elliott, with the mounted companies, was dispatched at midnight of the 12th to attack this place, while Colonel Miles, with the infantry and packs, was to march at the usual hour next morning. Captain Elliott got out of camp as secretly as he could, but was soon discovered, and signal fires were raised on his flank and front.

At noon on the 13th after a hard, hot and dusty march, Colonel Miles reached the lakes, and discovered a cloud of dust approaching from the south, which proved to be Lieutenant Averill with company K, Mounted Rifles, having in charge about 6,000 captured sheep. He reported he had a long chase after Indians, and that one of Captain Lucero's guides had killed one. Soon afterward Captain Elliott and the balance of the mounted companies arrived. There was not a sprig of grass about the lakes, and on being called up the captive said that over the hills to the northeast were corn fields, but he believed there was not water without they dug for it. After a continuous march for the cavalry of thirty and for the infantry of twenty-one miles, the corn-fields were reached early next morning, and the soldiers were put to enlarging the water holes made by the Indians. Before leaving camp in the valley at the mouth of the canyon the two women and three children previously captured were released.

About 3 o'clock on the morning of the 14th the Indians commenced firing on the pickets of the sheep guard, wounding four men with arrows, one of them mortally. As soon as the column advanced that morning the Indians collected and commenced firing on the rear guard commanded by Captain Elliott, but were handsomely repulsed. After marching twelve miles, what was thought to be a flock of sheep was discovered in front and to the right, and Colonel Miles dispatched Lieutenant Averill with his mounted company to capture them. On reaching the crest of the hills, two miles further on, Colonel Miles could see plainly that what he had mistaken for sheep were white rocks, and he then ordered Lieutenant Lane and his (the Colonel's) orderly, bugler Ezakiel Fisher, to recall Lieutenant Averill. After doing so the Lieutenant directed Fisher to cross over to the trail and await the coming of the command. Fisher, being a very absent minded man, neglected to do so, but kept on, and in a short march the column came to his dead body, pierced in the back with two arrows and stripped naked, except his gloves and shoes. Entering a narrow, wooded pass later in the day, Lieutenant Whipple was ordered to ascend to the left and Lieutenant Hildt to the right to protect the flanks of the column. Lieutenant Whipple soon scattered a large number of Indians concealed on the crest, doubtless intending to attack. That evening the command camped at the corn fields of Pueblo Colorado, and after dark the Indians again commenced firing on the camp, but at too great a range to do any damage, and when the pickets returned the fire, and one Indian was distinctly heard to grunt as if shot, the enemy retired.

On the 15th the command marched twenty-eight miles, back to Fort Defiance, the rear guard being repeatedly attacked by the Indians, of whom the troops killed two and wounded many, without injury to them-selves. The result of this scout was the killing of six Indians, the wounding of many, the capturing of four or five horses, six women and children, and the useful old man, and between five and six thousand sheep, and the destruction of several large fields of corn. The loss of the troops was two men killed and three wounded.

September 24th, 1858, Brevet Captain John P. Hatch, with company I, Mounted Rifles, fifty-eight rank and file, and company B, Third Infantry fifty-eight rank and file, under Lieutenant Whipple, left Fort Defiance at 10 o'clock at night for Laguna Negro, where, finding the country rolling and rough and the infantry unable to push on to the objective point in time to avoid the discovery of his approach, he left the infantry in charge of the baggage and pushed on, with fifty-two mounted men, to the wheat field and headquarters of Sarcillo Largo, the head chief of the Navajoes. He succeeded in conducting his command to within two hundred yards of the lodges of Largo's people before he was discovered by them, at 7 A.M. He immediately formed in column of fours, advanced to the front of the lodges, and dismounted his men within fifty yards of them. He was met by forty

Navajoes, armed almost exclusively with fire-arms. The engagement was quite hot for a few minutes when the Navajoes retreated; leaving six dead near the houses, and too certainly of those who escaped severely wounded one of these Sarcillo Largo himself, the head chief of the Navajoes, probably mortally. Captain Hatch's force was too small to allow it to be scattered in the thickets of oak near the lodges to look up the dead and wounded, or probably he could have reported a much larger loss to the enemy. He captured on the ground over fifty horses and a large number of buffalo robes, blankets, saddles, etc. many of which he caused to be thrown upon a wheat stack and burned. He then moved his command to open ground one mile and a half west of the wheat field, where he was joined by Lieutenant Whipple and the infantry, and after breakfast the little command returned to Fort Defiance, having marched fifty miles in twenty hours on one meal, dealt the enemy a staggering blow, and returned the command in as good condition as when it left headquarters.

September 29th, 1858, Second Lieutenant W. W. Averill of the Mounted Rifles, with a sergeant and ten men and four Mexicans, dashed into Chusca Valley, N.M., and after a skirmish with a band of Navajoes, captured nine horses and about one thousand sheep.

On the same date Lieutenant Colonel D. S. Miles of the Third Infantry commanding the Navajo expedition, again moved against the enemy from Fort Defiance and after a four day campaign returned to the post, having killed ten Indians, wounded many, and captured all of Kay-a-tana's camp equipage, eighty horses and 6,500 sheep. This great loss was inflicted upon the band to which the murderer of the Negro boy belonged. This was accomplished with the loss of two privates killed and one sergeant wounded. All of Kay-a-tana's wealth, aside from the sheep and horses captured, consisting of blankets, buffalo robes, corn, etc. was burned on the ground where captured.

October 3rd, 1858, Major Electus Backus, Third Infantry, was ordered from department headquarters to take command of a second column for the Navajo expedition, to consist of four hundred men, these to rendezvous at James, N. M. on the 15th, and commence a scout with forty days' rations, terminating its duties at Fort Defiance. Major Backus was instructed to make a through examination in and about Tuni-chey, from which point it was believed the Navajoes depredations upon the Abiquin and Jomez frontier. He was also instructed to "use the greatest possible exertion to destroy and drive from that part of the country every vestige of this troublesome tribe."

Finding that their people were being killed off almost daily, their flocks and herds captured and driven away, and still greater armies coming against them from different directions, while their Mormon allies who had incited them to hostilities against the government with at least an implied promise of assistance, had themselves sought safety in surrender, the Navajoes soon after gave up the unequal contest and begged for peace on any terms.

Even after the treaty of peace was signed this tribe remained sullen for a long time, but observed the stipulations of the treaty until some time after the great civil war began in 1861, when they against became troublesome, and were given an even worse whipping by the California Column of volunteers which came down through the Navajo country to New Mexico.

Chapter X

Death threat from Brigham Young (MOUNTAIN MEADOWS MASSACRE)

Note: I received this information (one week before publication) from Rev. Larry Preston from Butte, Montana, about his Great-great Grandfather Mr. James Gemmell who worked for Brigham Young, in the city of Zion for eleven years up to the end of September 1857, when he was told to leave Zion city or be killed. Mr. Preston thought this would be of some interest to the readers of this novel and about what his Great-great Grandfather over heard in Brigham Young's office about three weeks before the MOUNTAIN MEADOWS MASSACRE, and who said it and what was said.

James Gemmell, Pioneer Extraordinary

(First: some history on Mr. James Gemmell.)

From an obituary notice in the Dillon Tribune, April 9, 1881: "Died at Sheridan, Montana, Wednesday, April 6, 1881, at 11 A.M., after a lingering illness of many months, James Gemmell died at the age of 66 years.

> "Mr. Gemmell was one of the few men in this or any other country whose life from early manhood to old age, if fully written, would make a volume of such hairbreadth escapes as would be of interesting to old and young."

His life was certainly "unique," as he was at different times a soldier, prisoner, exile, escapee, sailor, fur trader, frontiersman, inventor, contractor, public official, farmer, pioneer and settler. Mr. Gemmell was also a patriot, believing sincerely in the cause of the Canadian insurgents and extending his aid to the greatest of his ability to further their cause. Known as "Uncle Jimmy" to his friends and neighbors until his death, it is said among his descendents that the nickname was given him by the Indians with whom he traded, and that Uncle Jimmy was made welcome in any Indian camp in Montana. There seems to have been no limit to his capabilities and his faculty to adjust to differing situations; during the period of his residence in Salt Lake, he went so far as to join the Mormon Church, and engaged in the practice of having more than one wife at one-time as was the custom in those days!

Not much is known about the early years of James Gemmell. He was born, 4 Feb. 1815 at Kilmarnook (Ayershire) Scotland. His parents were of the old Scotch Presbyterian faith. In 1821 the family moved to New York City where his father ran the Rob-Roy Hotel on Hammond Street near the East River. The hotel was much frequented by Scotch and Irish sailors, whose long yarns apparently filled him with the desire for travel and adventure while he was yet a young man.

The 1837 Canadian Rebellion

In 1835, at the age of 20, Gemmell went with his uncle to Canada, where they settled on a 200-acre farm about 15 miles north of Toronto. At about this time, the Irish in Canada were being incited to rebel against the Tyranny of England, and Gemmell soon identified himself with their cause. When open rebellion broke out in 1837, he joined the Patriot Army and was made a Lieutenant in a very short time. It was at the battle of Short Hill in June of 1838, while serving under Col. James Morreau, that he was taken captive by the British. Col. Morreau was among the captured group and was hung immediately.

Lt. Gemmell was sentenced to be hung in August of 1838. Before the death sentence could be carried out, the Governors of the upper and lower provinces disputed about questions of jurisdiction, the prisoners were referred to the Queen's Bench, and sent to Newgate Prison in England for further trial.

Lt. Gemmell tells about his capture and reception in England

Garret Van Camp, of New York…turned traitor at the Short Hills and was the cause of my banishment. Colonel Nelles had given me a pass to cross to the United States, as John M'Mullen, when a British Captain saw the mark of my sword-belt on the back of my coat. Van Camp, our comrade, was sent for and was faithless enough to tell them that I was Lieutenant Gemmell, of the insurgent service.

"After our arrival in England, we were for some months on board the *York Hulk*, off Portsmouth. We were then taken into a square crib called a wash house, stripped us naked, put into a big tub and well scrubbed by two convicts, our hair was sheared quite close, and we attired in the convict garb."

While in Newgate, Gemmell was visited by Daniel Webster and Caleb Cushing. Upon hearing the prisoners' story, these two great gentlemen promised to help the group as far as possible, especially since some of the prisoners were Americans. They took the matter to Lord Brougham who, in turn, argued their case before the highest tribunal in the land. He pointed out that the laws under which the captives were tried and convicted were invalid since they had not yet received the sanction of the Queen or Parliament. The original verdict was set aside and a new one handed down. The prisoners were banished to Van Dieman's Land (now Tasmania), there to endure penal servitude, for life.

In accordance with their sentence, Gemmell, with eleven others, was sent out from England, in the ship *Canton,* September 22nd, 1839. Gemmell was then 24 years old.

The ship arrived at Hobart's Town on January 16th, 1840, and the prisoners were taken about 100 miles into the interior to work on the road leading from Hobart's Town across the Island to Launcestown. In July 1840, the prisoners protested against the cruel treatment they were receiving; a round robin addressed to Sir John Franklin, Governor of the Island set forth that: "Fellows guilty of the foulest and most revolting crimes, were our overseers—that many of us had to work long and hard barefooted, with wretched food and worn out garments, toiling whether it rained or whether we were in a burning sun, with no place to dry ourselves when wet and weary, till the bell called us to be locked-up in our prisons at night." This petition only resulted in further misery for the already miserable prisoners. Sir John became incensed, had the men mustered, called them mutineers, ordered them to be dressed in magpie clothing—one leg and arm black, the other yellow—with a military guard to shoot them down if disobedient. They were then sent to the worst station on the island, called Green Pond. Unexpectedly, at Green Pound, they came under the supervision of Captain Erskine (son of Lord Chancellor Erskine and brother to the Ambassador from England, whose wife was an American). Captain Erskine sympathized with the prisoners, listened to their complaints and punished overseers who maltreated them. However, the station was broken up when Sir John learned of the situation.

The convicts' plight was alleviated in February 1842, when Secretary Lord Russell, learning of conditions at the penal colony called for certain changes in administrative policy. The convicts were allowed more freedom—each being given tickets by which they would be enabled to labor for their living, each man assigned to a township in the interior, beyond which he dared not go.

Although this new freedom was to lead to his eventual escape, Gemmell took a dim view of the situation as being little better than they had before. In his letter to the New York Plebian after his escape in 1842, Gemmell writes:

"These townships extend perhaps ten miles by five, and contain, on the average, perhaps thirty landowners, who will unite to pay the poor captive just what they please, as he can go nowhere else; and if he demand a settlement, they may assert that he was saucy; and, any two of them being magistrates, can send him to the chain-gang for a year, or otherwise coerce him. Redress is a thing not to be thought of. I have seen enough of this. If I were now a Van Dieman's Land 'relief captive,' I would gladly exchange for slavery in Virginia as far preferable."

"It is impossible for me to describe the state of society in Van Dieman's Land. Nine-tenths of the people are convicts—the men are bad enough. Some of their crimes are so revolting that I forbear to name them; and as for the London prostitutes, they are there in the thousands, and infinitely worse than the worst of men. Virtue itself would soon be contaminated in such a polluted atmosphere. There are no distilleries, but money is plentiful, and Van Dieman's Land is the most remarkable place for drunkenness I ever saw. The American and the Canadian prisoners established temperance societies at which some of our ablest men lectured and a very few of the English convicts joined us."

"The law is administered in a very summary and severe manner, Sir George Arthur would sometimes sign eleven death warrants in a morning, and see them executed too."

The entire story of his two years on the island would doubtless fill the pages of a fair sized book. That Gemmell did not spend a longer time there is a credit to his ingenuity and courage and the ability to see his chance and take it. The story of his escape—"so far as prudence will permit"—follows:

"Mr. Norris, a police magistrate and formerly butler to Sir George Arthur, had received a large tract of land, which he was anxious to clear. I persuaded him that I could build a stump machine if I had the model from Mr. Woodman, of Maine, who lived beyond Hobart Town; and such was his anxiety, that he gave me a passport to that place, in which the ship that brought me, the place where I was born and tried, with my complexion and height, the color of my hair, eyes, checks and eyebrows, the shape of my mouth, were faithfully inserted. My police ticket was Number #1474; there being there on the island that number of prisoners whose sir-names begin with G."

"The passport (which I yet have) was in direct contempt of the public orders of the British Government; and the moment I exhibited to a Mr. Gunn, the superintendent, a letter from several of the prisoners asking for their own clothing, that shrewd Caledonian suspected my design, arrested and gave me in charge to an armed constable, I being still attired in the conspicuous magpie grab in which I had reached the capital. I was ordered to be taken back into the interior immediately, was handcuffed, and being accompanied by several male and female criminals thither bound, set out on my weary journey. At noon, the constable took off my handcuffs-that I might eat, when I seized his musket, declared that, I was off for the bush, and disappeared. In the night I left my hiding place, crept into Hobart Town, told some white-souled American tars (sailors) my unfortunate history and they required no coaxing to perform the part of honest men. The victim of oppression found deliverers, and entertains no fear whatever that John Tyler, President of the United States, will send him back again, but would rather hope that the friendly aid of this great nation through its executive, will soon effectually relieve those who yet groan in bondage, and restore them to their free and happy homes."

Thus was James Gemmell delivered from bondage back to the free world, which meant so much to him. Nor did he forget his comrades, companions and friends of the Patriot Army, as subsequent events soon show. In the same letter from which the above passages were taken, can be found an insight into the heart and soul of the man. This portion I am about to quote, I consider both inspiring and enlightening. There is in this one paragraph, of all the writings of James Gemmell which I have studied, a singular quality and a beauty of expression which I would liken to other great documents of freedom which make up the backbone of our American System.

"In concluding I would again entreat every friend of humanity to endeavor to get the United States government to interest itself in the matter of my unfortunate comrades. It is visionary to assert that the exertions of a few dozen of men, un-influential, unconnected with politics, and worn down by pain and privation, could have the least effect in changing the destiny of Canada. And if not, why continue to torture them? But let us avoid all frontier movements—the best weapon in the hands of this great republic, with which to revolutionize the world, is surely a strict adherence to the wise, just and honest policy, which carries in its train, prosperity and peace. That is the true way to create admiration for institutions theoretically liberal and free. Had we succeeded in Canada in 1837, independence would have followed, but not war with America."

War would only insure the oppression and captivity of tens of thousands who are happy in the bosoms of their families, would inflame the bad passions of two great nations, speaking one language, and capable, under such forms of government as they may respectively choose to uphold, of enlightening, benefiting and blessing mankind; but it would not soothe the grief's of the orphans and widows, the fathers and brothers, of those manly hearts which now beat on a far distant shore with fond and anxious confidence and hope that they will yet find opportunity, friends and delivers in the land of Washington."

Freedom and the westward call

Aboard the whaling vessel, Gemmell was treated kindly by the officers and crew, and worked his passage before the mast to New Bedford, Massachusetts. The news of his escape preceded him, and he was met at the wharf by friends who aided him and saw him aboard a steamer for New York.

Since he was the first American to escape from Van Dieman's Island, he was considered quite a celebrity and treated very kindly. Before the vessel could dock, he was taken aboard a yacht' by two men who insisted on him to going with them. They proved to be Horace Greeley, editor of the New York Tribune, and a James Gordon Bennett, editor of the New York Herald. Upon landing, they ushered him to the Astor House and informed him that he was their guest for as long as he chose to remain. He was treated royally (new cloths and money) at the Astor House, where he stayed for a week, repeating his story to many visitors and writing his letters to the newspapers.

After seeing his family, he then headed for the Canadian border in an attempt to locate some of his companions of the Patriot Army, intending to stop at Salina to see friends of prisoners from that neighborhood.

Since he could not re-enter Canada, he decided to help the patriots by going into business in Michigan. He engaged in business in Detroit, was successful, his gains going mostly to help the Patriot cause and other Canadian exiles like himself.

While in Detroit, he fell in love with a Miss. Harriet Fitzgerald, the daughter of ex-senator John Fitzgerald. They were married, had two children and lived very happily until the time of her death in 1847.

West to Utah and Montana

James Gemmell started west from Detroit in 1844 when the controversy between the United States and England over the Oregon boundary question was at fever point. The cry of the day was "54^0-40' North or fight." Gemmell was certain that it could only be settled by war, and decided that he might be of some service to the United States if he journeyed to the Oregon Territory, and join the U. S. Army. By this means he could satisfy his desire to enter into the conflict, and by serving on the side of the United States, he could repay England for their hospitality that they inflicted on him and his friends.

On his journey westward, he became acquainted with Jim Bridger, and that colorful old mountain man excited Gemmell's imagination with his tales of the wealth to be gained in the fur trade with the Indians on the Yellowstone. Bridger also told him vivid tales of that remarkable area at the headwaters of the Madison where there was to be found wonderful spouting-springs and other miraculous oddities of nature.

Before Gemmell had crossed the continent to the Pacific coast, the boundary dispute was settled, and having no further incentive to go on to Oregon, he decided to join Bridger's band of frontiersman and regain the fortune he had spent in the rebellion.

William F. Wheeler, former librarian of the Montana Historical Society, presents the tale of Gemmell's journey through Yellowstone, as told to him by the old man at his home in Sheridan, a few months before his passing.

"Mr. Gemmell said: 'In1846 I started from Fort Bridger in company with old Jim Bridger on a trading expedition to the Crows and Sioux. We left in August with a large and complete outfit, went up Green River and camped for a time near the three Tetons, and then followed the trail over the divide between the Snake River and the streams, which flow north into Yellowstone Lake. We camped for a time near the west arm of the lake and here Bridger proposed to show me the wonderful spouting springs at the head of the Madison. Leaving our main camp, with a small and select party, we took the trail by Snake Lake (now called Shoshone Lake) and visited what have of late years become so famous as the Upper and Lower Geyser Basins. There we spent a week and then returned to our camp, whence we resumed our journey, skirted the Yellowstone Lake along its west side, visited the Upper and Lower Falls, and the Mammoth Hot Springs, which appeared as wonderful to us as had the geysers. Here we camped several days to enjoy the baths and to recuperate our animals, for we had had hard work in getting around the lake and down the river, because of so much fallen timber which had to be removed. We then worked our way down the Yellowstone and camped again for a few days rest on what is now the reservation, opposite to where Benson's Landing is now."

"From here we crossed the present Crow Reservation and made our winter camp at the mouth of the Big Horn, where we had a big trade with the Crow and Sioux Indians, who at that time were friendly towards each other. The next spring we returned with our furs and robes, passing up the Big Horn River and over the mountains to Independence Rock and thence home."

Apparently it was on these trading expeditions among the tribes that Gemmell received his nickname "Uncle Jimmy." The story, handed down to his descendents, is that Uncle Jimmy was known and welcome in the camp of any and all of the Indian tribes in the Montana area. If true, it is certainly a tribute to the personality of the man and his ability to get along with people, for some of the tribes, notably the Blackfeet, and the Sioux, were not exactly friendly with each other and were prone to treat as an enemy any trader who traded with an enemy tribe. However, as far as actual evidence is concerned, it has only been noted that he traded with the Crows, the Sioux, and later with the Flatheads. (As early as 1850 he journeyed into the Flathead country in the Bitterroots, and as far north as what is now Missoula County.)

In 1847 he placed his children under the care of his wife's relatives, and started in June for Oregon, with his own outfit of six horses and two wagons, his aim being no more than to reach the coast. With him were William Gansen and Dr. Toby. This same Dr. Toby later became a noted practitioner near the Cascade Mountains in Oregon.

Some of the adventures that befell the party during the three months before they reached Salt Lake are interesting and worth noting. In attempting to swim the Platte River, his friend (Gansen) drowned. When they reached Fort Laramie, they found over 300 emigrants and joined them for the trip further west. Some of the men folk, where not very friendly to each other as a Mr. Cox shot his own brother while quarreling over a game of cards. He was tried by a Citizens' court-martial, found guilty and shot on the spot. Another man killed his partner, was also tried at once, and hanged because of the near by trees. "Such was law and order." Mr. Gemmell was the hunter for the train and in one day killed six buffalo.

Upon reaching Salt Lake City in1846, tired and worn out, and still with no further aim than to go west, Gemmell took a contract with Brigham Young to dig 100,000 rods or (312.5 miles) of ditch digging at $1 per rod. Here Gemmel shows his ability as an inventor. He designed and constructed a machine with which he completed the contract. He also built a scraper, for use in road construction, which was used to full advantage later.

He remained among the Mormons for eleven years, contracting and working on public works. After the State of Deseret was formulated and became an actuality in 1849, Gemmell took a fairly active part in the building of Salt Lake City. At the assembly held on September 14th, 1850, it was stated under the passage of the Act Incorporating the Perpetual Emigration Company, that "Robert Pierce employ Mr. Gemmell with his improved ditching machine and scraper to work under his direction upon the Public Works."

In the minutes of another assembly on October 5, 1850, it is stated: "Mr. Gemmell was appointed Supervisor of Roads in place of Robert Pierce, who resigned."

Gemmell also built the bridge at Ogden, and the one across the Jordan River (in which Brigham Young designed both) and helped in laying out the city of Salt Lake, and inaugurated the planting of Cottonwood Trees in the Salt Lake Valley.

Gemmell then joining the Mormon Church and married the sister of Bishop Hendricks of the Hot-springs Bath House, who bore him two children.

In Brigham Young's office
(The Mountain Meadows Massacre affair)

In the last few days of August of 1857, Gemmell was in Brigham's office to talk over some city business that needed his attention, as Bishop Jacob Hamblin was talking to Brigham; Gemmell over heard Hamblin talking about a wagon train from Arkansas that was a few days out from the City, this is when Gemmell heard Brigham say, "If I was in command of the Legion (Nauvoo Legion), I would Wipe Them Out." After a short time later Hamblin left the office by himself. Gemmell confronted Brigham with what he had just heard, and this is when Brigham Young told Gemmell, that this was a *"military matter"* and it was none of is affair, and say nothing to no one or he would be arrested for treason against the State, and put to *death*.

Gemmell did not agree with some of the Mormon tenets, or their dealings with the gentiles—especially with the emigrant trains which were putting into Salt Lake for provisions on their journey west, by over charging them, for so little.

For the next few weeks he stayed close to home, with his *guns* at the ready. Then one day Gemmell received word of a wagon train massacre, attacked by Indians, and it was the wagon train from Arkansas.

Gemmell was then obliged to leave Salt Lake City or face *Death*. He journeyed to Montana by himself as fast as he could, leaving his two wives' and children behind. He would come back from time to time over the years to make sure every one was fine.

It wasn't until the spring of 1864, that he was able to bring Susan and their children to Ruby Valley where they settled on a ranch of 160 acres, near the present town of Sheridan, in Madison County.

As having abandoned the Mormon faith, James Gemmell was obliged to leave his other wife, Hannah, in Utah. Hannah had been the widow of Susan's late brother Isaac Brown (killed by Indians in Nevada), before she married James Gemmell in 1852. Hannah and Gemmell had four children. (Also married by Brigham Young.)

Brigham Young and Gemmell were very good friends, until right up to the end. Brigham was the one who married Gemmell to Susan Mariah Brown, in 1850, they had 12 children and now 160 acres in Montana which to run and play.

A list of Gemmell's Wives.

Harriet Fitzgerald-Gemmell, 1-child.

Edith Richards-Gemmell, no-children.

Elizabeth Hendricks-Gemmell, 2-children.

Susan Mariah Brown-Gemmell, 12-children

Hannah Davis-Gemmell, 4-children.

(James Gemmell, was the only child.)

Spelling clarification

This spelling-used in Scotland in the 1720's by the family, Gemmill.

This spelling-used in New York in 1812 by the family, Gemmell.

This spelling-used in Canada, and by the British in 1837, Gemmill.

This spelling-used in the 1860's by some of his other children in Salt Lake, Gammell.

Time passes quickly,
like the wind,
on your cheek!

MORMON AND INDIAN WARS;

THE MOUNTAIN MEADOWS MASSACRE,

AND OTHER TRAGEDIES AND TRANSACTIONS

INCIDENT TO THE MORMON REBELLION OF 1857.

TOGETHER WITH THE PERSONAL RECOLLECTIONS OF A

CIVILIAN WHO WITNESSED MANY OF THE HORRIFYING SCENES

DESCRIBED.

BY

CAPTAIN JOHN I. GINN.

ABOUT THE AUTHOR

Steven Farley likes to write about Western History, looking for new adventure around every turn in the bend of the river. Farley's ancestors in 1887 after crossing into Wyoming from Missouri en-route to Oregon to homestead. They started the long uphill pull to Fort Laramie and on up the North Fork of the Platte to where it meets the Sweetwater River. Here they followed up the Sweetwater to it's beginning and up over South Pass with an Elevation of 7,550ft.

Down the west side of the pass they went to Fort Bridger near the Utah border. The Forts were a welcome change for the travelers as they could talk to other people and replenish their depleted food supply. Farley, was told even Prairie Dog stew became a delicacy.

From Bridger the trail turned North West again toward Fort Hall. It was along this area where the Mormons had installed a ferry across the stream and were charging to cross. The fee was too high to please the travelers so they decided to follow along the bank until a place to cross was found so the Mormons offered to lower the price but by now it was too late. They refused and went their way and did indeed find a crossing with no toll to pay.

Printed in the United States
33757LVS00004B/125

9 781410 743633